THE HANDYMAN

THE HANDYMAN

A GRIPPING DOMESTIC THRILLER

GABRIEL PIERCE

DARK CORNER PUBLISHING

Trade paperback ISBN: 979-8-9996112-1-5

 Formatted with Vellum

PROLOGUE

We had given a psychopath the keys to our home, but I was the only one who realized it.

I heard him downstairs at that very moment. His heavy footsteps thudded around the first floor as he worked on another "fix" in the house. Granted, there were plenty of repairs needed in the old home, and I'd been forced to admit to my mother that I couldn't handle them all myself despite my best intentions.

But he wasn't there to fix things.

He was there to break us.

How could I get him out of there?

I sat on the edge of my childhood bed, door locked, clutching my phone in my clammy hands. But there was no one to call for help.

I was on my own.

Below me, I heard his drill whine to life. The sound vibrated through the floorboards, through the walls, through my bones. He was installing something. Always installing something. Smart locks. Security cameras. Motion sensors. Each "improvement" tightening his control, hurling us deeper into a web I couldn't yet see clearly enough to escape.

Mom thought he was a blessing. "Such a nice young man, Jessie. So helpful."

That was the genius of it—he'd made himself indispensable to her while making me look paranoid, unstable, jealous of the attention he gave her. Every concern I raised, every warning I issued, only proved his false narrative: *Poor Jessica. That divorce really did a number on her. She's not thinking clearly.*

The drilling stopped. In the silence that followed, I heard his footsteps again—slower, deliberate. Moving toward the staircase.

Coming up.

My breath caught in my throat. I'd installed a new lock on the bedroom door, but he had a knack for always finding a way inside.

His footsteps reached the landing, thudded along the hallway. Paused outside my door.

The handle turned, testing. Once. Twice.

Then his resonant voice came, eerily pleasant: "Jessica? I'm going to need access to your room soon. Just want to take some measurements."

He didn't say what for. He never did anymore. Just vague mentions of "enhancements" and "safety" and "taking care of things."

That was somehow worse than a specific lie—the refusal to justify or explain. As if my questions didn't matter. As if I didn't matter.

As if he'd already won.

I pressed my hand over my mouth to keep from screaming.

The worst part of it all?

I was the one who had hired him.

A FEW WEEKS EARLIER...

1: JESSICA

One word burned in my mind as I stared at the house: *Failure.*

I squeezed the steering wheel of my Honda Accord. It was a dreary Friday afternoon in October, and until that week, I would have been at my marketing director job in Atlanta, winding down the workweek and finalizing plans for the weekend—plans that would have involved my husband, Mitch.

Things had changed so quickly I felt as if I'd suffered the mental equivalent of whiplash.

Last Friday marked my final day at the company where I'd climbed from entry-level marketing coordinator to director over twenty-one years. My role—my expertise, my relationships, my entire professional identity—could apparently be replaced by artificial intelligence. The severance package felt like a consolation prize for becoming obsolete.

Cardboard boxes consumed every inch of my car's interior. They towered on the passenger seat in precarious stacks. Mountains of them filled the back seat, blocking my rearview mirror. More boxes stuffed the trunk until the Honda's suspension groaned under the weight. The storage unit held everything else—furniture and keep-sakes too painful to look at, wedding photos I couldn't bear to destroy but refused to keep around.

I had brought only the essentials for starting over. Today, I was moving back into my mother's house.

My phone buzzed in the dashboard mount.

It was Mitch calling. On the phone, his name popped up as, *Cheater.*

Mitch had a knack for knowing when I'd hit an emotional pothole, maybe the residual effect of living together for five years and being married for three, a telepathic bond or whatever.

With that said, he could also be amazingly clueless.

"Why would I want to talk to *you*, of all people, right now?" I said aloud to the phone as it continued to chime.

The call died, dumping him into voicemail. Before I could exhale, it started ringing again. Classic Mitch—convinced persistence would wear me down.

I didn't pick up. Instead of leaving a voicemail, he followed up with a text. I plucked the phone out of the holder to read the message.

I'm sorry, Jess. I know you'll never forgive me, and I deserve that, but I'll always love you. I'm here for you whenever you need me, okay?

My thumb hovered over the BLOCK button. I had a strong impulse to do that, right then. The only thing that kept me from it was the possibility that he might have some legal matter to tell me about at some point.

Our divorce had been finalized only three days ago. The judge's signature was literally still wet on the papers.

I also thought of responding with a curt, *I'll never need you again.* But I knew Mitch. That would only encourage him to try to change my mind for the hundredth time, and he would swamp me with more texts and calls.

The best response—which I knew would drive him nuts—was no response whatsoever.

I deleted the message and shoved the phone back into its mount.

The driveway stretched ahead, leading to Mom's house, my childhood bedroom, my spectacular failure. The weight of it pressed down on my shoulders, threatening to crush what remained of my dignity.

2: JESSICA

Mom's house looked as beat up as I felt.

She lived on the edge of Newnan, in an area that was still mostly rural despite urban development pushing at the borders of town. It was a farmhouse-style home, two stories, with an attached two-car garage. The white clapboard siding needed fresh paint. One green shutter dangled at a drunken angle from the front window. Gutters drooped under the weight of rotting leaves, and kudzu strangled the foundation walls.

Dad never would have let the house fall apart like this, I thought.

But Dad had died nine years ago. I had visited Mom at the house plenty of times since then—Mitch and I lived about an hour away, in Dunwoody—but until that day I had never turned a critical eye on the condition of Mom's home. That was the difference between breezing in and out for visits and moving in to live there again. I had a new perspective on just about everything.

It's temporary, I had promised myself. Staying with Mom for a few months would keep me from blowing through all the severance money I'd gotten from my job, allow me some breathing room to get back on my feet. Mitch and I hadn't bought property together (thankfully), and the lease expired that month on the townhouse we'd rented. He had already moved out and I saw no reason to stay. The place held too many painful memories.

Like coming home early from work to find Mitch and his coworker romping in the bedroom . . .

I shoved the thoughts out of my mind and parked next to Mom's Toyota Camry in front of the garage, her vehicle blanketed with fallen leaves. I grabbed my purse from atop the box on the passenger seat and got out of the car.

Thunder rumbled overhead, and the air tasted metallic with approaching rain.

As I walked to the house, I noticed the veranda could use painting, too. The current coat peeled off the wooden railing like sunburned skin.

The porch floorboards creaked and groaned underneath my footsteps.

A wasp circled the hanging lantern above the front door, trapped in its own endless orbit. Spiderweb cracks covered the lantern's glass as if someone had used it for batting practice.

The door swung open before I could find the doorbell—which appeared broken anyway, its button hanging by corroded wires.

Mom stood in the doorway, wearing an Atlanta Braves sweatshirt, black sweatpants, and bright pink Crocs. Her salt-and-pepper hair twisted into an efficient bun, reading glasses perched on her nose. Even in casual clothes, she exuded the authority of the high school English teacher who'd once made students fear her red ink pen slashing across their essays.

But there were signs of age, too. The deepening crow's feet at the edges of her eyes. The multiplying strands of gray in her hair. The tiredness in her gaze—I knew Mom struggled with insomnia most nights, which she confessed hadn't started until Dad died.

"Hey, Jessie," Mom said.

Her arms enveloped me before I could respond. The embrace lasted longer than our usual polite hugs, her slim body radiating warmth that seeped through my jacket. She smelled of lavender soap and chamomile tea.

"Thanks so much for letting me stay here, Mama," I said, unwittingly using my childhood name for her.

"Of course, baby. My door is always open to my firstborn. I'm excited to have you back under my roof."

I had a younger brother who lived in Chicago, Lawrence Junior. He was three years younger than I was and had accomplished everything I hadn't. I heard the eldest child was supposed to be the trailblazer, but somehow at the age of forty-three I was divorced, unemployed, and moving back into my childhood bedroom—not "failure to launch," but "launched, crashed, and burned."

I stepped out of her arms, but she kept a hand balanced on my shoulder and assessed me from head to toe, her head tilted to the side.

"You've put on weight," she said.

I felt my chest tighten, but I forced a casual shrug. "While I'm here, I plan to start running again."

"Do you?" Her mouth twisted into a sardonic smile. "I hope you actually follow through this time, Jessie. You can't afford to let yourself go completely. You're still young enough to attract a decent—"

A shrill beeping sound cut through her words, echoing from somewhere inside the house.

"Wait, what's that noise, Mom?"

Her shoulders sagged like deflated balloons.

"All right, come on in. We might as well contend with this mess now."

3: JESSICA

As Mom ushered me inside, I couldn't help noticing the state of things. When I used to visit her with Mitch, Mom would go through the trouble of straightening up the house. Now, with me moving in to stay, she'd apparently abandoned all pretenses.

I saw two or three coffee mugs sitting on the table in the front room, alongside a couple of plates littered with crumbs. A foot-high stack of old newspapers stood on an end table. Amazon package boxes of every conceivable size cluttered the hallway—some opened, some sealed, all creating a cardboard maze that screamed of compulsive online shopping.

We passed by the kitchen. I glanced in there and saw dishes scattered across the countertops and table, as if she'd hosted Thanksgiving dinner the night before and walked away mid-cleanup.

The air hung thick and sour, layered with the smell of forgotten garbage and something else—the musty scent of a house surrendering to neglect.

Does Mom actually live like this? The question twisted my stomach. I'd never suspected, never looked past her carefully orchestrated performances during my visits.

One crisis at a time, Jess.

I followed her upstairs. The steps groaned underneath our footsteps, and the banister wobbled at my touch, an accident waiting to happen.

In the upstairs hallway, we gazed upward at the source of the mechanical shrieking: a smoke detector crying for new batteries like a dying bird.

"How long has this been beeping?" I asked.

"I can't tell you. It's become like white noise to me."

I gaped at her. "Seriously, Mom? Why didn't you replace the batteries? Haven't you done that before?"

"Your husband took care of it last time. Can we call him?"

"*Ex*-husband. And I'll handle this myself. Where's the ladder?"

Mom's eyes went blank for a beat. "In the garage?" She frowned, then brightened. "Or did I lend it to Carol next door? I'll have to ask her."

"You don't sound too sure."

"That's where it should be, I think, in the garage." Her eyebrows pinched together as if the effort of remembering caused physical pain. "I'll look for some batteries."

Shaking my head, I went downstairs and into the garage. I hadn't explored that area in a long time and wasn't prepared for the archaeological dig that awaited me.

More junk. A lot more. Enough dusty exercise equipment to furnish a small gym: a treadmill, an elliptical machine, a stationary bike, a rolled-up yoga mat, and assorted dumbbells. Boxes full of kitchen gadgets—oddly specific things like mango peelers and egg cookers. Dad's riding mower was buried beneath moldering cardboard towers, and his tool collection still occupied its designated corner, everything exactly where he'd left it nine years ago.

No wonder she doesn't park her car in here.

But there was no ladder.

I found Mom ransacking kitchen drawers when I returned, her movements increasingly frantic. She turned as I approached, hand raised in triumph.

"Found 'em!" She wagged a box of Duracell batteries at me.

"The ladder's not in the garage. There's lot of *other* things in there that I won't get into right now, but no ladder."

"Are you sure?"

I nodded. "When was the last time you used the ladder, Mom?"

"I changed a light bulb a couple of weeks ago."

"Where?"

"In my bedroom."

"Will I find the ladder in your bedroom?" I asked, watching her face closely.

"I wouldn't do that," she said in a sharp tone. "Why would you say such a thing, Jessie?"

Because you're forgetting things, Mom, and that's another reason why I wanted to move back home—to watch over you.

"Let me go back upstairs," I said, leaving her question unanswered.

The ladder stood exactly where I'd predicted—propped in the master bedroom corner beside the windows, probably abandoned weeks ago after that light bulb change. My stomach clenched in a cold knot.

As I carried the ladder out into the hallway, Mom arrived at the top of the staircase.

"Where was it?" she asked.

"In your bedroom."

"I didn't leave it there. Someone must've moved it."

"Someone? You live alone."

Mom glanced away from me, and I suddenly felt as if I were embarrassing her, and I didn't want to do that.

In a gentler tone I said, "Do you have the batteries, Mom?"

She dropped the box into my palm. I positioned the ladder underneath the smoke detector.

Perspiration coated my palms as I ascended the rungs. Mitch had always handled home maintenance issues, and I felt a little queasy with the prospect of what lay ahead: not only tasks like this but a thousand other things I'd have to figure out on my own somehow.

But I was more than capable, I assured myself.

I damaged a fingernail prying the detector's cover loose and bit back a curse.

"I miss having your father here," Mom said in a low voice, one hand resting against the ladder. "He was so good at taking care of things in the house. Junior was, too, and so was your Mitch."

"He's not *my* Mitch anymore. We're divorced, officially—I've got the papers in the car."

"Have you ever considered giving him another chance, Jessie?"

I looked down at her. "He cheated on me, Mom. I saw it with my own eyes."

"I understand how upsetting that betrayal would be, but your father wasn't perfect, either—far from it." Running her fingers through her hair, she let out a soft chuckle. "But listen, your father and I stuck together and worked through the rough patches. Marriage is work. Children in your generation abandon ship much too easily."

My jaw tightened. I'd heard this lecture from her before.

"I don't need to go running to Mitch for anything anymore," I said. "I can handle things myself."

"It's okay to ask for help sometimes, so long as you're asking the right people."

I tuned out her words and focused on the job at hand. I finally popped in the new battery, and the annoying chirping stopped assaulting my ears.

"All done." I climbed down from the ladder and forced a smile. "No man required, see?"

Her answering smile flickered and died, her gaze drifting to some distant place I couldn't follow. These episodes had multiplied during our recent phone calls and visits—moments when her mind seemed to disconnect from reality. The last time I'd mentioned one of these mental lapses, she'd given me a tongue-lashing I would never forget.

I am fine, Jessica Marie. Don't worry about me. Worry about your own broken life.

That reprimand still stung. But I was worried about her, too.

What else would I notice now that I was living here?

4: JESSICA

My first priority was transforming my childhood bedroom into a functional office and living space.

I'd rarely wandered into my old room since I had moved out over two decades ago. Now, knowing I'd sleep here indefinitely, the space seemed like a museum exhibit dedicated to my younger self.

Everything was . . . smaller. The full-size bed looked like a prison cell cot compared to the California king I'd shared with Mitch, the ceiling seemed lower, the windows were narrower than I remembered, and the old oak-veneer furniture seemed like it belonged in an infant's room.

How was I going to adapt to this?

Grin and bear it, Jess, I thought. *You can handle it.*

I set down a moving box next to the desk that I hadn't sat at since high school. This would be my new workstation for a freelance marketing consultant business I'd launched, but it was a far cry from the office I'd enjoyed at my old job: a glass-walled oasis with a stunning view of the Atlanta skyline.

"I fixed it up for you," Mom said from the doorway. "I dug out your old high school yearbooks and other mementos and set up some pictures for you I thought you'd like, Jessie." She smiled, but it looked bittersweet. "I want you to feel comfortable."

I straightened, put my hands on my hips, and looked around. I noticed old photographs and documents—things I hadn't seen in *years*—had been framed and positioned on various end tables throughout the room and on the walls. A photo of me and Dad at the beach on Tybee Island, which must have been taken when I was about five years old, both of us intent on constructing a sandcastle. Me posing onstage with the high school principal at my graduation, diploma in hand. A handwritten essay titled "What I Will Be When I Grow Up" written in my careful fourth-grade penmanship, back when I was obsessed with becoming a veterinarian. (Why hadn't I pursued that? It would have been safe from AI.)

Tears welled in my eyes. "This is so sweet, Mom. Thank you."

"I confess, I'm getting a touch sentimental in my old age." Mom gave me a lopsided smile, shrugged.

"I love it," I said, and meant it. I gave her a hug. "And seventy-two isn't *that* old."

"Tell that to my creaking knees, honey." Her eyes got that faraway look again. "Seems like yesterday I was your age, worried about English department politics and raising two children. Where did all the years go?"

It was a question I often asked myself, too, especially now. But it was too depressing to dwell on.

"I've got to get things settled in here," I said. "This will be the fancy digs of JT Consulting."

"Is that your new business?"

I'd explained my entrepreneurial plans during at least three recent phone conversations. Another memory lapse, or had she simply tuned me out?

"Last year, I registered the LLC and drew up an initial business plan," I said. "Everyone's supposed to have a side hustle, right? I didn't do much else with it, though."

"You're not planning to look for a new job in corporate?" She sounded horrified.

"I'm going to focus one hundred percent on growing my own company, Mom. I've already got some leads right here in town. Remember Dr. Danvers?"

"Our family dentist?"

"Yup, and he admits he doesn't know diddly-squat about social media marketing. He's facing a lot of competition from these new dental chains and wants to improve his visibility. I've set up a meeting with him for next week."

"That sounds promising, Jessie," she said, but her attention had flicked to her iPhone. She tapped and swiped the screen. "Junior's posted new photos of the kids. They're so *cute*. Have you seen the new pictures?" She thrust her phone toward me.

"I'll look later. I need to finish unpacking."

A while later, after I had unpacked everything and made progress on arranging the new look, I crossed the hallway for a bathroom break. Mom had vanished downstairs, probably scrolling through more grandchildren photos that reminded her of everything I'd failed to provide.

As soon as I flushed the toilet, water surged upward like a geyser verging on eruption. Frantic, I searched for a plunger. The narrow cabinet under the vanity held only spare toilet paper and ancient bottles of Mylanta.

I flung open the door and raced to the staircase. "Mom! Where's the toilet plunger?"

"What's wrong?" Her voice drifted up from the living room.

"The toilet's flooding!"

Mom thundered up the staircase, moving faster than I thought she could manage. "Did you use the toilet across from your room? I meant to warn you—it's finicky."

You've gotta be kidding me. Why is everything in the house broken?

As Mom rushed upstairs, I snatched open the linen closet door in the hallway, grabbed an armful of towels, and ran back to the bathroom. My heart hammered. The last thing I needed was a plumbing crisis on my first day back home.

But I found, much to my relief, that the water had receded without spilling onto the tile floor. The flush mechanism thingy had been delayed, but worked.

"Thank goodness it didn't spill over," Mom said from the doorway, her cheeks flushed. "I haven't gotten around to hiring a plumber to repair the toilet." She rubbed her fingers together. "It would be expensive, Jessie, and I'm on a fixed income. Be careful about using this one, okay?"

"I bet we could fix it ourselves," I said, making a mental note to check some YouTube videos on home repair.

"If your father was still with us, certainly. That man could fix anything. But it's only us, Jessie. I'm all thumbs, and *you* broke a fingernail switching out that smoke detector's batteries." She chuckled and sauntered away.

"At least I tried," I mumbled to her back, feeling sixteen again.

Behind me, the toilet gurgled ominously.

5: JESSICA

"How does it feel being back home, Jess? Are you adjusting? Or is your mom driving you completely insane?"

The following Wednesday, I met my best friend, Claire Wilkins, at Sweetie's Café in Peachtree City. Before I'd relocated to Newnan, midweek lunches with Claire had been impossible—the hour-long drive from my Buckhead office made casual meetups a logistical nightmare. Claire lived in Fayetteville, and this bistro with its exposed brick walls and rustic wood tables served as our perfect halfway point.

Claire had claimed a corner booth beneath a gallery wall decorated with local landscape paintings. She wore her signature business casual uniform: a satiny cream blouse that probably cost more than my monthly car note, perfectly pressed black slacks, and low heels that somehow managed to look both comfortable and elegant.

Although I was my own boss, I'd dressed as if I still reported to a corporate office—old habit. Lounging around in hoodies and sweatpants while I tried to build a business felt frivolous.

I probably looked like a shabby sister beside Claire's effortless glamour. We'd been tight since freshman year at Newnan High, but she'd always possessed a physical attractiveness that turned heads and broke hearts. Long, thick hair that tumbled in luxurious waves to her shoulders, big, sparkling eyes that made her look like a doll, a smooth complexion that required little makeup and defied age.

Her manicure gleamed. Her one-and-a-half-carat wedding ring twinkled in the light, complemented by a tennis bracelet that could probably fund my business launch. Her blue BMW X7 was parked in the spot directly outside our window.

I didn't begrudge Claire anything. Until recently, I'd done well in my career, too. Claire was an estate law attorney at a small firm outside Atlanta, but apparently, she was well-compensated, especially considering her husband was a high school teacher and varsity football coach. Over the summer, she and hubby spent a week on the Amalfi Coast, posting enviable pics on her Instagram page.

"How is it with Mom?" I asked. "Let's say I'm learning a new level of patience."

"How so?"

Mulling over my answer, I stabbed the grilled chicken salad with my fork. I'd resisted ordering the club sandwich and kettle chips that I'd craved. Mom's observation—*you're putting on weight*—still rattled like a stone in my mind.

"Her memory is worse than I realized," I said.

"I'm sorry. I know how tough that can be."

Claire's father had suffered from Alzheimer's.

"But do you know what shocked me even more, Claire? The condition of the house. It's falling apart. I never truly noticed until now."

Claire bit into her club sandwich—the exact entrée I'd denied myself. She'd probably burn off every calorie during her evening treadmill session. Exercise addiction was her only vice—if you could call disciplined self-care a vice.

"She's been living there all alone," Claire said. "It's a large house for one person to manage, and she's getting up in years . . . Probably hasn't been noticing things for the reason you mentioned."

"There's a lot to do there. I mean, a lot. She's a borderline hoarder on top of all the broken things."

"Oh." Claire wrinkled her nose.

"It's amazing what you see when you move in. All the little things." I pressed my fingertips against my temples where a slight migraine was building. "I'm trying to get this business running, but I've still got to be a one-woman renovation crew."

"Have you ever heard of HandyHelper?"

"Is that one of those contractor apps, like Thumbtack or Angie's List or whatever it's called now?"

Claire sipped her sweet tea, another indulgence I craved but had to pass on. Too many carbs.

"Similar, yes," she said. "I've used it plenty of times. You know Joe can barely change a light bulb without reading the user's manual."

Claire had been married to her college sweetheart, Joe, for going on twenty years. They'd met at the University of Georgia over in Athens, which I'd attended also, but she managed to snag her future husband while she was there, too. She seemed to have the marriage, career, and kids thing all figured out. Was there a secret guide I hadn't stumbled on yet?

"I don't know about hiring contractors to work in the house," I said. I rubbed my thumb across my damaged fingernail. "I've had bad experiences with those guys. I'd rather do things myself. Give me a YouTube video and I'm good, girlfriend."

"But when will you have time for all of that? You need to focus on growing your business, Jess. Let a professional handle the household repairs. I've had good luck with HandyHelper and the prices have always been reasonable."

"Wow, you ought to do a commercial for them."

"I'm only spreading the word. Every contractor on the app undergoes a background check, too, if that's a concern."

"Fine, to make you happy, I'll get it now." I grabbed my iPhone from beside my water glass, located the app in the store, and clicked the GET button. "There, see?"

As I directed the screen toward her, my phone buzzed with an incoming call. It was Mitch. Again.

"Who is Cheater?" Claire asked, her perfectly sculpted eyebrows arched. "Let me guess: Mitch."

I put the phone face down on the wooden table, where it continued buzzing like an angry hornet.

"He's only calling out of guilt," I said. "He knows he ruined a good thing. But I've moved on."

"Good for you, girl," Claire said. She twirled the straw in her sweet tea, her eyes twinkling. "We haven't properly celebrated your freedom yet. We need to plan a night out somewhere fabulous."

"I'd like that."

"And soon. We need to get you back out in the dating pool." Claire smirked. "There's an app for that, too, Jess—or so I hear. I wouldn't know personally." Mischief glimmered in her eyes.

I laughed. "No, thanks. I'm taking a *looong* hiatus from men. Don't trust 'em. Don't need 'em."

"Well, they do have a certain practical purpose occasionally." Claire chuckled and took another sip of tea, ice cubes clinking against glass.

I flipped over my phone. Mitch had called twice—he never called just once—and followed up with a text message.

I'm here, Jess. In case you ever want to talk. I still love you, babe.

When would it sink in that I had booted him out of my life and moved on?

I deleted the message and shoved the phone into my purse.

6: JESSICA

Friday, two days after my lunch with Claire, my workday was humming along perfectly—until disaster struck.

To start, I had a morning meeting with Dr. Danvers, our longtime family dentist, at his office in downtown Newnan. He knew nothing about how to leverage social media to grow his client base, having only a sad-looking Facebook page and no presence at all on other platforms. He signed a contract on the spot for a monthly marketing package and wrote me a check—my first actual earnings for my business.

I probably would have taken the rest of the day off to celebrate, but I had other meetings booked. A late-morning Zoom call I took in my bedroom with a new prospect, a real estate developer, went fabulously well. They wanted me to visit their office to do a more detailed presentation, and we booked a time for next week.

I was on a roll.

High from that meeting and needing to prep for my next one in an hour with yet another lead, I hurried across the hallway, used the toilet, and rushed back into my room, immediately plunging into meeting prep. I had a killer PowerPoint deck I wanted to walk

24

through with my next prospect, but it needed a few final tweaks before our discussion.

My stomach growled, but I tried to ignore it. I was fasting intermittently, so food would have to wait until dinner. I'd stepped on the scale that morning and discovered I'd shed two pounds since last week—the motivation I needed to stay on track.

A few minutes later, I heard Mom scream from downstairs, her voice muffled through the closed door behind me.

"Jessie!"

I rocketed to my feet, panic surging up my throat. Had Mom fallen and hurt herself?

I flung open the door—and that was when I saw it.

A glistening tide of water spilling out of the bathroom, creeping across the threshold and into the carpeted hallway. I heard the toilet still gurgling softly.

Oh no . . .

"Jessie!" Mom shouted again. I heard footsteps pounding up the staircase.

I crept to the bathroom door, pushed it all the way open, and flicked on the light.

Water submerged the tile floor, probably an inch or more already. It continued to cascade from the toilet bowl.

That stupid toilet. Why had I used it? I hadn't been thinking . . .

"Water's coming through downstairs!" Mom said, out of breath as she reached me. "It's dripping into the kitchen from the ceiling vent!"

I froze, the magnitude of the crisis rendering me speechless.

"Call someone!" Mom shrieked.

"I've gotta shut it off," I said, though I had only a vague idea how to do that.

I waded into the water, cold waves sloshing over my sneakers. There had to be a way to shut off the water pumping into the toilet, to stop the flooding.

Kneeling, I saw a thin rubbery tube protruding from the floor and snaking upward into the toilet. Water had to be flowing through there. Grimacing, I leaned forward, stretching my arm around the toilet bowl, my fingers getting wet, until finally I felt a smooth plastic knob.

I tried to twist it, but it wouldn't budge, and the water kept coming.

"You don't know what you're doing!" Mom shrieked. "Call someone!"

She was right, but I wasn't ready to give up that easily.

I twisted the knob in a different direction, and that did nothing except damage another fingernail. I bit back a curse.

Come on!

And finally I *pulled* the knob—I don't even know where the idea came from to try that. Pure desperation maybe.

The surge of water stopped.

I straightened, my knees creaking.

"I shut it off," I said, turning back to face my mother with my accomplishment. But she wasn't there.

I sloshed through the water—*did we even have enough towels to sop up all this water?*—and hurried downstairs, my shoes squeaking across the staircase.

I found Mom in the kitchen. She had placed a large stainless steel stockpot in the middle of the floor. A steady trickle of water dripped from the ceiling air vent and plopped into the pot, and I saw dampness spreading like fast-growing tumors across the beige-colored ceiling.

Hands on her hips, Mom stared at the growing water stains and the dribbling stream as if a steady gaze could force them to stop.

"I warned you about that toilet, Jessie," she said, not looking at me. "I told you it was finicky."

My face got hot. "Why didn't you ever get it fixed?"

"Why didn't you fix it, Miss 'I Can Do Everything Myself'?"

"I've been a little busy, Mom. I'm trying to a launch a new business, in case you haven't noticed."

"Meanwhile, we'll be living with mold above and below. Do you know how quickly it starts growing, Jessie? Within *twenty-four hours*."

My head throbbed. Could the timing of this disaster have been any worse?

"Well, I'll call someone," I finally said. "I'll make sure all of this is taken care of. I promise."

"At last, a reasonable step." Mom nodded, her lips pressed together tightly, her jaw rigid. I recognized that look of hers. In her mind, I knew she had pinned the blame for this incident squarely on me.

"I'll do it now," I said.

Upstairs, I grabbed my phone off the desk. Just recently, Claire had recommended the HandyHelper service, and that seemed as good a place to start as any.

I typed in our zip code. Then in the "Help needed" search box, I typed in "Plumbing, flooding," not quite sure how to characterize what had happened, but I immediately received a score of results, profile photos of men—they were all men, I noticed—alongside reviewer ratings.

The top result was a very good-looking guy named "Lance C." He had over two hundred ratings with a 4.8 stars average.

I clicked on his profile link to see more details.

Native of Newnan, Georgia. Twenty-five years of professional experience as a general contractor and handyman. Prompt, friendly, professional. I can fix anything. Licensed and bonded.

His reviews were stellar. But there was something vaguely familiar about his name, if not the face. If he was a native of Newnan, like I was, and had been working in the field for twenty-five years, he was probably about my age. I had most likely seen him around town or in school.

I didn't like to make impulsive decisions, but I couldn't spend hours reading reviews of these guys and weighing who to call. This guy clearly had experience, people liked him, and he was local.

I clicked the MESSAGE button and crossed my fingers.

7: JESSICA

Forty-five minutes later, after Mom and I finally had mopped up the water in the bathroom as best we could, I heard a vehicle arrive in our driveway.

During our text messaging exchange inside the HandyHelper app, where I described our issue in more detail, Lance had promised he could get there within an hour. His punctuality had to be a good sign, I hoped.

The water had, at last, stopped dribbling from the ceiling vent, but it had filled most of the big stockpot. Stains had spread across a wide swath of the kitchen ceiling.

I didn't want to think about how much all these repairs were going to cost. Mom said she had homeowner's insurance and could file a claim, and I promised to tackle that onerous task for her, too. I didn't want to see that look of accusation on her face anymore.

Why didn't you fix it, Miss 'I Can Do Everything Myself'?

I'd had to reschedule the sales call I should have been on at that very moment. Life happens. Maybe this was only a speed bump, though, and if this guy was as good as his reviews, I could get back to my business soon and let him handle this flooding issue.

"He's here already?" Mom said. "Goodness, so prompt!"

She practically vibrated with anticipation. A man was coming to solve our problems—her favorite kind of rescue scenario.

I lifted the curtain at the front window and glanced outside. Lance had arrived in a gleaming black Mercedes-Benz Sprinter cargo van. He had backed into our driveway.

Another good sign: He had the right vehicle for the job. I'd taken a couple of minutes to research flood repair, and learned that big, heavy equipment was required to dry the impacted areas: industrial-size fans and dehumidifiers. Our house would sound like an airplane hangar for the next few days.

Lance climbed out of the van. My breath caught in my throat.

This man belonged on magazine covers, not crawling under sinks.

He was tall, with broad shoulders tapering to a narrow waist. His hair was cropped in a stylish fade, his jaw clean-shaven and angular. He wore well-fitted jeans and a crisp white work shirt that displayed muscular forearms. Every movement radiated confidence, strength.

If Lance and I had been in high school together twenty-five-plus years ago, there was no way he'd looked like *this* back then.

He glanced toward the house, and I jerked away from the window like a guilty teenager.

I smoothed down the front of my blouse and checked my reflection in the hallway mirror. Due to my Zoom calls on camera that day, I was dressed professionally, except for my shoes—I had changed out of my damp sneakers and into a pair of Crocs. My hair looked fine, but sweat from the cleanup effort had smudged my makeup.

You're being silly, Jess. He's here to work on the house—not to take you on a date.

He rang the doorbell. Nervous energy fluttered through my chest as I opened the door.

"Miss Jessica Taylor?" Lance flashed a dimpled smile that showcased perfect white teeth. "I'm Lance Cutler, your handyman."

His voice resonated with warm bass notes and the faintest

Georgia drawl. I barely processed his words because his eyes demanded complete attention—penetrating yet kind, radiating intelligence and something else I couldn't identify.

"Hi," I said. Ugh. I sounded froggy.

He extended his hand, and my fingers vanished within his massive grip. Despite his obvious strength, he applied only gentle pressure.

"You haven't aged a day," he said.

I blinked. "Excuse me?"

"I went to Newnan High School, too. Class of 1999. You were one year behind me, but I remember you very well." He winked. "I'd asked you out to prom, once, junior year. You turned me down flat." He snapped his fingers for emphasis.

"I did?" Heat flooded my face.

He laughed—a rich, infectious sound that seemed amused rather than bitter.

"But you hired me today, and I'm appreciative for a second chance," he said. "I guarantee complete satisfaction with my work. May I come inside?"

I stepped aside with an awkward welcoming gesture. His greeting had rattled me. He'd asked me to prom? How could I possibly forget rejecting someone who looked like this? I'd dated occasionally during high school but never seriously, and I certainly wasn't popular like Claire. Guys like Lance didn't notice girls like me.

As he passed, his cologne enveloped me—a blend of cedar and warm spices applied with perfect restraint. Masculine without being nauseating.

"If it isn't Mrs. Taylor," Lance said, approaching Mom. "If I didn't know any better, ma'am, I'd think you and your daughter were sisters."

Mom giggled and blushed. "Lance Cutler! Of course, I remember you! You mowed our lawn when Larry was recovering from his back surgery."

"Indeed, I did. I had a modest little lawn care enterprise back then, before Pops taught me the ropes as a general contractor—that was his profession." Lance's tone shifted to a somber note. "Please accept my belated condolences on Mr. Taylor's passing. He was a good man who treated me fairly."

"Thank you," Mom and I said in unison.

But I had questions: How did he know Dad had died? Had he done research on us? Heard it through the local grapevine? Dad's death was nine years ago, hardly a recent event. The precision of Lance's knowledge of us was peculiar.

"I remember your mother," Mom said. "She used to manage a restaurant in town, didn't she?"

"Mother passed into glory three years ago." Lance bowed his head. "It's only me and Pops. Pops is in assisted living now, unfortunately; Alzheimer's, you know."

We murmured appropriate condolences while I studied his performance. Everything felt slightly rehearsed, too polished for spontaneous conversation.

Maybe I was being too hard on him. I had a longtime aversion to home contractors, and this entire situation had put me in a foul mood.

"So." Lance clapped his hands and surveyed us both with professional authority. "I'd like to assess the situation and get to work. Would you gracious ladies please give me the tour?"

8: JESSICA

Determined to keep an open mind with Lance, I led him to the kitchen, with Mom bringing up the rear behind him. I was grateful that I'd cleaned all the dishes last night, washing them by hand because the dishwasher (of course) was glitchy. I would have been embarrassed to bring a stranger inside the house and let them see dirty dishes heaped in the sink—it was one of those tasks that Mom neglected now that I was there.

The dampness on the ceiling looked as if it had spread further, but the dripping from the ceiling vent hadn't resumed.

Lance clicked his tongue like a robot. "Yes, I've seen cases exactly like this before. I'll take my moisture readings in a bit, but I can assure you, the material is thoroughly soaked. Mold will start growing within hours if we don't begin mitigation procedures. We can't delay."

"That's what I told Jessie," Mom said.

I shot Mom a look. Why was I the villain here? The toilet was broken when I moved in.

"Let's go upstairs," I said.

I felt Lance's attention on me as we climbed the rickety staircase

—a feeling like a tickle at the back of my neck. When I glanced over my shoulder at him, he averted his gaze, but it made me self-conscious, again, about my appearance, which then annoyed me. Why did I care about his opinion of my looks?

You haven't aged a day.

"Here's what started it all." I pointed at the old toilet in the tiny bathroom. "When I used it, I'd forgotten it was *finicky*, as Mom had said."

"Jessie promised to fix it herself," Mom said. "We see how *that* turned out."

I glared at Mom.

"We're dealing with it now, okay?" I said.

"Two inches of toilet water later."

Lance cleared his throat and stepped forward. He studied the toilet with theatrical concentration, like a doctor scrutinizing a patient on an exam table.

"This model was defective when it rolled off the manufacturer's assembly line," Lance said.

"You actually know that without seeing the serial number or anything?" I asked.

"In my line of work, over the decades, I've seen thousands of models," he said. "It's remarkable that it's functioned as long as it did. This one is original to the house, correct?"

I looked at Mom, and she nodded. "Thirty-five years. Larry replaced the handle and some sort of mechanism in the tank a couple of times, but it kept on working nicely until about a year ago."

"I'll swap it out with a new one," Lance said. "I've got a Kohler Highline in my van."

Whatever it was, it sounded expensive.

"How much would replacing the toilet cost, versus repairing it?" I asked him.

"I'm giving y'all the family discount for all my work here, so it doesn't matter," Lance said.

"How kind of you." Mom beamed at Lance. If he'd offered her birdseed from his palm, she would have pecked it out.

I folded my arms across my chest. "Why do we get the family discount? What's the catch?"

"Jessie, for goodness' sake, don't look a gift horse in the mouth," Mom said with an eyeroll.

Ignoring my question with a bland smile, Lance crouched beside the toilet, appearing to examine the shutoff valve. "Whoever stopped the water flow demonstrated quick thinking under pressure. Who managed that?"

"I did." I raised my hand. "Honestly, I wasn't sure how it worked. It's sheer luck that I shut it off."

"You were willing to try when water was flooding the bathroom. That says a lot about you, Jessica. Grace under fire."

"Thank you. I hope I acted soon enough to minimize some of the damage."

"We'll have the verdict soon." Lance straightened. "I'll go out to the van and fetch my ladder. Be right back, ladies."

We returned downstairs.

"He's perfect," Mom said, once Lance was outside. "And he's giving us a discount! I know we're planning to file a claim with my insurance, but I want to keep the bill as low as we can."

"Still not sure why we're getting the alleged family discount," I said. "He completely ignored my question."

"We get it because we have a history, Jessie. Didn't you hear how he used to cut our grass when he was a boy?"

"There's always a catch," I said.

Mom clucked her tongue. "You sound exactly like your father sometimes."

But I couldn't get a good read on Lance, and it bugged me.

He seemed highly competent. He brought back a steel ladder, which he set up in the kitchen, and scanned a moisture meter—some little handheld gadget—against the ceiling, confirming that the wood was soaked. With practiced authority, he talked about removing light fixtures and using the holes as entry points for his big fans, to minimize demolition damage to the ceiling. I couldn't question his professional skills.

But something about him seemed off. He seemed a little too eager to please, with this family discount thing, and his claim about asking me out in high school still irked me. It was twenty-five years ago, sure, but I *know* I would have remembered a guy like him trying to put the moves on me.

You don't trust him because he's a member of the male species, Jess. Admit it.

But he was here in the house, he had the proper equipment, and he seemed to know what he was doing, so what was I going to say? Leave, because I'm not sure I trust you? He was here to do a job, nothing more. We couldn't afford to drag out this situation while I auditioned one contractor after another. The threat of mold spreading, within a few short hours, was real.

Lance headed upstairs again to take a moisture reading in the bathroom, too, and I followed him. Mom had escaped to her garden, content to tend to her homegrown vegetables now that a qualified man was handling our crisis.

On his knees—he had slipped on a pair of knee pads, like a baseball catcher—Lance swept his meter device across the tile. I observed him from the doorway.

"The floor is completely saturated up here as well, as I expected," he said.

"Wonderful. Will we have to replace the tile, or can your machines dry it out?"

"Too early to say for sure. I'll set up a couple of fans and my dehumidifier up here, and I'll take readings over the next few days. If we can get the moisture levels down to a safe threshold, the floor can stay. If not—"

"You'll have to rip out the tile."

He nodded. I blew out a heavy sigh. The hits just kept coming.

He rose to his full height, broad shoulders unfolding as he

straightened. Suddenly I realized how close we stood in the narrow space. I retreated several steps into the hallway.

Smiling, Lance stepped forward, too, pausing at the edge of my personal comfort zone.

"Is that still your bedroom?" He nodded at the door across the hallway.

The way he said *still*—as if I'd never left, never built a life elsewhere—made my gut clench.

"I moved back only a week ago. It's temporary. I'm here to help Mom." That was the story I was telling everyone who didn't need to know my full bio: I'm here to help Mom. Not: My life is in shambles and I need a safe space to regroup.

"Divorced?" he asked, a thin smile playing on his lips.

"Happily," I said, raising my chin.

"Is you ex someone I might know from school?"

"Nope. What about you?" I noted his bare ring finger.

"Widowed. My wife passed away ten years ago. Cancer. She was the love of my life. After her, I've no interest in remarrying."

"I'm sorry for your loss. Did she go to Newnan High?"

"We never had children, unfortunately," he said, deflecting my question. "But the upshot is that I've plenty of time to devote my full attention to my clients. I guarantee complete satisfaction. Even though you rejected me in high school, hiring me as your handyman was the best thing you could've done, Jessica."

He laughed good-naturedly, but why did he bring up the rejection again? Did it still annoy him?

And why did he keep ignoring my questions?

Lance strode down the hallway with quick, purposeful steps. I hurried to catch up.

"What's the timeline for everything you need to do here?" I asked.

Lance paused at the staircase, where he tested the steadiness of the wooden banister. It wobbled, of course. Like a quick draw gunslinger pulling a pistol, he whipped a screwdriver out of his tool belt and tightened the loose screws on the railing.

"Oh, thanks for that," I said. "I was going to get around to fixing that, too."

He gave me a dubious *sure you were* look, but said, "In cases like yours, it's usually a minimum of three days to reduce the moisture to a safe level. Once that's done, I can replace the tile in the bathroom, swap out the toilet, drywall the kitchen ceiling wherever needed, and repaint it."

"Then we're looking at what? Three or four days?"

"In the best-case scenario."

"This sucks." I dragged my fingers through my hair, exhaling. "I've started working from home. It's going to sound like a construction zone in here."

"The equipment makes a racket but it's necessary to eliminate the mold threat." He cocked his head. "What kind of work do you do?"

"I've got a marketing consulting business. I worked in the field for over twenty years," I added quickly, not sure why I felt the need to explain my experience to him.

"Nice. I've built a strong business network here in Newnan and all over. Maybe I can throw some referrals your way." He twirled the screwdriver in his long fingers, his eyes gleaming.

"Along with the family discount, huh? Thanks, but I don't need any more favors."

"Everyone can use a favor sometimes."

Slow your roll, guy. I crossed my arms over my chest.

"Anyway, like I was saying, I was planning to take calls here in the house." I glanced back toward the bathroom. "Things were going well until this catastrophe hit us today."

"I'll make this experience as painless as possible for you and your mother, Jessica, but I suggest you find an alternate location for your business calls while my equipment is operating."

I sighed again.

"On another note, there's plenty of other projects to tackle in this home," Lance said. He gestured to the railing he'd tightened. "Inside, and out, I've noticed. You can focus on growing your business, your mom can enjoy her garden, and I'll take care of everything that needs to be addressed here—I can fix anything. For a very reasonable price."

"Let's tackle one project at a time," I said.

"You want to assess the quality of my work before you commit to a longer-term arrangement." He clicked his tongue. "I respect that. It says a lot about your character."

Another compliment. He was full of them, wasn't he?

"I've had bad experiences with contractors," I said.

"Fair enough." He nodded. "By the time I'm done with this first job, you'll be thrilled for me to keep working here for you and Mrs. Taylor. I guarantee it."

9: JESSICA

L ance was right about one thing: The industrial-grade fans and dehumidifiers were entirely too noisy for me to work from home while they operated. The machines rumbled like jet engines in the kitchen and bathroom. After Lance departed, promising to return tomorrow morning to measure progress, I packed up my laptop and a few other items and got ready to leave myself.

I checked in with Mom before I left. During nice weather, she would spend hours in the fenced backyard: working in her rather impressive vegetable garden (I had not inherited her green thumb), or lounging in her creaky rocking chair on the faded wooden deck while she read classic literature, skimmed social media on her phone and called old friends, and bought more junk online.

She had fallen asleep in her chair, a worn paperback copy of Shirley Jackson's *We Have Always Lived in the Castle* lying on her lap. I touched her shoulder, and she stirred.

"I wasn't asleep," she said, and yawned. "I was only resting my eyes."

I smiled at this oft-repeated explanation of hers. "I'm heading out to get some work done. The airport hangar inside is too distracting."

She nodded. "Thanks for hiring Lance to come take care of us. You're stubborn as all get-out like your father, but you always end up doing the right thing."

"Gee, thanks, Mom."

"We're fortunate he had availability on such short notice, and for such a large project."

"Sounds like his machines are doing most of the work."

"But he has all the proper equipment for the task at hand." She pushed up her glasses on her nose, her eyes glimmering. "He comes from a good family as well. Why didn't you two hook up in school? He says you rejected him?"

Of course, Mom would have overheard that part of my exchange with Lance. Her memory might occasionally be faulty, but she didn't miss anything when it came to my romantic life.

"I've gotta go," I said. "Please send me a text if you need anything while I'm out."

"It could be Providence, you hiring him," Mom said with a soft laugh as I turned away. "A second opportunity for a connection . . ."

I'd decided to visit the public library. I hadn't been inside the building since high school. Renovations had given it a futuristic look: an automated book return system and study pods that looked like something out of a sci-fi movie.

The place was deserted on a Friday afternoon. I found a quiet, isolated corner and set up my laptop, and hauled out the things I really wanted to dig into: my old high school yearbooks, which Mom had dutifully saved and set aside in my bedroom.

Lance clearly was bugged by my rejection. I was bugged being unable to remember him at all.

I started with freshman year. The laminated covers crackled as I opened the book.

He said he was a year ahead of me. I flipped past the freshman class, studiously avoiding my own hideous photo—braces and bad acne—and found the sophomores.

His last name was Cutler. I didn't find his photo where I expected it to be, and at the end of the section, his name was printed in a "Not Pictured" list. He must have missed Picture Day.

Next yearbook, then.

My sophomore portrait looked much better. The braces were gone, and I'd started on a course of acne treatment with a new dermatologist that cleared up my skin. This was one of the better pics I'd taken as a teenager.

But no Lance Cutler. Again, he'd landed on the "Not Pictured" list for his junior year.

On to next year, then, which was when he claimed he had asked me out. I skimmed past my photo—*still looking good, Jess*—and flipped through the senior class.

"Oh," I said aloud.

There he was at last.

Like all the boys in the senior class photos, he wore a suit. He wore enormous glasses—the lenses were almost comically out of proportion to his face—and his head was totally bald. He was grinning, and it was obvious a couple of his teeth were crooked.

Talk about the ugly duckling growing up into a swan. I had to admit: My sixteen-year-old self would have turned down this guy cold.

But you still would have remembered it, if only because of how he looked.

Idly, I paged through the yearbook. There was a section full of random candid photos, and I stumbled across another one that showed Lance hugged up with a plain-looking girl in front of a hallway locker. She and Lance embraced like a couple. Despite my rejection, he had found someone to love.

I went back to the class photos. Lance's girlfriend was also a senior: Melody Rockwell. I didn't recognize the name, but she was a year ahead of me.

Was this young woman the love of his life who had passed away?

I grabbed my phone and googled: "Melody Rockwell, Newnan."

The only notable search result was a jarring one: an obituary dated from ten years ago.

I skimmed it. It was the same Melody Rockwell from my class yearbook—she was from the class of 1999. No cause of death was noted, however.

Even more notable: There was no mention of a marriage to Lance Cutler, and his name wasn't listed anywhere. If she was his wife, the love of his life, why wasn't he named in the obituary?

10: JESSICA

The next day was Saturday, and I'd slept terribly. The industrial fans and dehumidifiers had droned throughout the night like a fleet of small aircraft, their relentless hum penetrating even the foam earplugs I'd jammed into my ears around midnight. Every time I drifted toward sleep, the pitch shifted—a bearing catching, a motor cycling—and snatched me back awake.

Around eight, I dragged myself out of bed, but I weighed myself on the scale. Okay, making progress. Feeling slightly more motivated, I threw on my workout clothes and sneakers.

Downstairs, Mom looked as exhausted as I felt. Dark crescents shadowed her eyes, and she stood at the coffee maker in her tattered green bathrobe, staring at the dripping brew with the hollow expression of someone who'd been awake all night.

"You look how I feel," I said, shouting to be heard. "This equipment is awful."

"It's for a good cause," Mom said. She gave me a quick once-over, her gaze lingering on my workout clothes. "You're going to exercise?"

She sounded surprised. As if she didn't believe me when I first told her I was going to start exercising again.

"I've lost three pounds now since I moved in," I said. "I need to keep it up. I'll be at the high school, on the track."

"Good for you." Mom poured her coffee and added two heaping spoonfuls of sugar and a glug of cream. "What time is our Lance coming?"

Our Lance? What was he, a member of the family now?

"He didn't say, but he's supposed to come sometime today to check the moisture levels." I pulled out my phone. "I'll ask him now."

He had provided his business phone so I could contact him outside of the HandyHelper app. I opened a text thread and typed: *Morning. What time are you coming to check in?*

The message showed as delivered immediately. I waited, watching for the three dots that would indicate he was typing a response.

Nothing.

"Tell him I'm making banana bread today," Mom said. "He mentioned yesterday that banana bread was his favorite."

"When did he mention that?" I asked, but Mom had already shuffled toward the living room, coffee cup in hand, moving like a woman twenty years older.

I grabbed my keys and headed out to my car. The morning air was crisp and clean, a welcome change from the machine-processed atmosphere inside the house. I sat in the driver's seat, windows down, breathing deeply.

My phone sat silent in the dashboard mount. No response from Lance.

He's probably still asleep. Normal people sleep in on Saturdays.

I expected a quick response, but I didn't get one. I drove to the high school, about a ten-minute trip, and stepped onto the outdoor track.

The track was already populated—a handful of serious runners doing interval sprints, a few older couples power-walking together, a young father pushing a jogging stroller. Weekend warriors like me trying to slow the decline of age.

I settled into a brisk walk, my playlist pumping motivational pop into my AirPods. Five thousand steps. That was the goal. Manageable. Achievable. Something I could actually control.

I was halfway through my third lap—about twenty-five hundred steps—when my phone buzzed against my hip.

I'm here now.

I stopped walking so abruptly that the woman behind me nearly crashed into my back. She veered around me with an annoyed huff.

I scowled at the phone. Couldn't he have messaged me when he was on his way—not already there? I needed to be there myself during his visits. I was the one who had hired him.

My thumbs darted across the screen: *I'll be there shortly. Next time can you please let me know in advance when you plan to visit?*

His reply was immediate: *Your mother is here. Isn't she the homeowner?*

Heat flushed my face. I stood there on the track, other exercisers flowing around me, my hands shaking.

I wasn't going to get into an argument with this man via text messages. This was stupid.

I made it one more lap—barely—before I gave up and headed back to my car. My fitness app informed me I'd completed only thirty-eight hundred steps. Failure, again.

I drove back home.

11: JESSICA

Lance was climbing into his van as I turned into the driveway. Upon seeing me, he paused at the driver's-side door and waved.

It was still hard to reconcile how he looked today with his senior yearbook photo. He definitely wasn't one of those guys who had peaked in high school.

I parked behind Mom's car and got out. On the drive home, I'd rehearsed what I was going to say, but he started talking before I could speak.

"I'm all done for today, and I've got great news." He flashed a radiant smile. "The moisture levels have dropped to thirty percent. I expect we'll need only another twenty-four hours of mitigation, and then I'll take away my machines and give you back peace and quiet."

"Let's get back to your text message: My mother is the home-owner, but *I* hired you. I'd like to be here when you visit."

Lance's smile never faltered.

"Some of my clients provide me with a key," he said. "There's no need for either of you to be present while I'm working."

"I want to be here, Lance," I said. Why did I need to say that again? "In the future, please get in touch with me before you visit."

"You like being around me, hmm?"

I stammered. "What?"

He chuckled, good-naturedly.

"I'll see you tomorrow, Jessica. Will you be attending church with your mother at First Baptist?"

He was throwing random comments at me, keeping me off balance. How did he know what church mom attended?

Mom told him, Jess. That's how.

"Please stop by after eleven," I said. "Text me when you're on your way. *Please.*"

"Yes, ma'am." He saluted, and I got the sense that he was mocking me. But then he said: "By the way, you're looking real good. Whatever dietary and fitness changes you've made are working well for you, Jessica. Keep it up."

He smiled and got in his van. I watched him drive away, my heart rate elevated.

You're looking real good.

Inside the house, I looked for Mom. I spotted her through the glass doors leading to the deck. She was out in her garden.

I didn't feel like talking to her then and hearing more compliments about Lance. Although my workout had been cut short, I could have used a shower. I headed to my bedroom to strip out of my gym clothes—and found the door half-open.

Had I left it open before I went to the track?

Frowning, I stepped inside.

I gave the room a once-over. I didn't see anything out of place. Was my imagination running away with me?

I got undressed, shrugged into my house robe, and went to my mom's bathroom to take a shower. With the machines rumbling away in the bathroom with the broken toilet, I needed to use her shower until the work was done.

Afterward, I returned to my room and opened a dresser drawer to get fresh underwear, the drawer squeaking as I pulled it out.

Someone had moved my panties.

I'd folded several pairs and tucked them on the left side of the drawer, while keeping T-shirts on the other side. The panties now sat on the right side and the T-shirts on the left.

He's been in my room. Going through my things.

My heart knocked again.

Quickly, I checked the rest of the room to see if anything else was out of place. Tellingly, only my underwear had been moved.

I dressed and went outside. Mom was examining the vegetables in her garden.

"Hey, Jessie. How was your workout? You missed Lance. He says the drying is going well!"

"Was he in my bedroom, Mom?"

Mom gave me a fuzzy look. "Why would you say that?"

"Someone moved my underwear."

Mom stared at me, as if still not comprehending.

"I put them on the left side of the drawer. When I just looked, I found them on the right side."

"Are you certain, Jessie? I know how fussy you are about your clothes, but why would this busy man enter your private quarters simply to shift around your panties?"

Hearing the words from her made me sound paranoid.

"Were you inside when he was working in the house?" I asked.

"I let him in, we chatted for a bit, and while he did his checks, I came outdoors to work on the garden. He stopped out here before he left only a short while ago." She frowned at me. "Are you all right? You look frazzled."

"He was in my room," I said again.

Mom only clucked her tongue. "You and your OCD. Just like your father, you know. If I touched one of his tools or if I merely *thought* I had, he'd chew me out. Half the time he'd misplaced those items on his own."

Was I being paranoid? I had an almost visceral sense of violation at the idea of a stranger pawing through my clothing, but could I be imagining things? Had I misplaced the underwear myself and not realized it?

"He's harmless, dear," Mom said. "I'd love to have him return to do more work, after he completes the current project. There are so many repairs . . ."

"Absolutely not." I shook my head adamantly. "We'll find someone else for anything else we need. He's not the only handyman in town."

Mom scowled at me.

"And from now on, until his job is over," I said, "I'm locking the door."

12: JESSICA

"Do you remember a guy from high school named Lance Cutler?" I asked Claire later that afternoon.

We were on a FaceTime call. Claire took my call from a familiar spot: striding on the treadmill in her home gym, the phone sitting on the machine's console and giving me a direct view of her face. Perspiration beaded her forehead, but she still managed to look glamorous.

I sat in my car in the driveway. It was too noisy inside the house for me to communicate clearly, and I didn't dare make this call within eavesdropping range of my mother.

"Lance . . . Cutler?" Claire asked. She was barely panting, though I knew from experience that she cranked up the treadmill to over four miles per hour even when walking.

"He was a year ahead of us." I had brought the yearbook outside with me and had already propped it open on my lap to the right page. I angled the phone's camera over Lance's senior photo. "This is him."

"Ugh," she said, lips curling. "No, Jess. Definitely not. I'd remember that face. Why?"

I hadn't told Claire anything about our recent toilet flooding disaster. I quickly brought her up to speed.

"Finally, you took my advice for once and used HandyHelper," Claire said.

"I always take your advice."

"You married Mitch when I warned you he had a wandering eye."

"Name a man who doesn't have a wandering eye. I'll wait."

"Semantics." Claire puffed out a breath. "You know what I mean. So Lance from high school is working in the house and doing a decent job despite his less-than-flattering high school pic. What's the issue?"

"He says he asked me out to prom back in school and I turned him down. I have zero recollection of that."

"It was over twenty-five years ago."

"I feel like I would remember. It's not as though guys were swooning over me back then. You got that sort of attention, but I didn't."

"Do you think he lied about it, to make you feel guilty?"

"Well, he looks like a movie star now."

"Oh, is that so? I may have to check him out on HandyHelper." Interest glimmered in her eyes. "And having a hot handyman is a problem, Jess?"

"He's been flirting with me, sort of. He seems a little too fascinated."

"You're divorced, remember? A good-looking guy shows interest and that upsets you?"

"I think he went through my underwear drawer when I was gone. I found things moved around. He would've had an opportunity."

"Oh," Claire said in a muted tone. Her eyes hardened. "Gross."

"Yeah," I said. "Exactly. Mom thinks I'm delusional. She loves the guy—I forgot to tell you, he used to cut our grass, back in the day when Dad was on disability. And she knew his mother, which is like a major bonus with her."

I heard Claire adjust the incline, saw her head float upward in the camera frame.

She said, "Mom's got the warm fuzzies about this Lance guy, and meanwhile, you're getting a stalker vibe."

"I hope I'm not overreacting, but I've got a touch of OCD about how I arrange my clothes."

"Ain't that the truth. I remember when we roomed together at UGA. If I so much as nudged a pair of your shoes one centimeter, you'd freak out."

"I want to show you this, too." With a Post-it note, I had marked the other page in the yearbook that featured the candid photo of Lance and Melody Rockwell in a lover's embrace. I panned the phone to show it to Claire.

"I've no idea who that girl is, either," Claire said.

"You're useless. I thought you knew everybody in school."

"I knew everybody worth knowing. Count yourself lucky I knew you, girlfriend."

Yeah, Claire could be conceited sometimes, too.

"Her name is Melody Rockwell," I said. "She died ten years ago —I found the obituary. Lance mentioned to me that his wife died ten years ago. I assumed his late wife and this girl in the picture were the same person, but Lance wasn't mentioned in Melody's obituary."

"Then it's probably *not* the same person, Jess. More to the point: Why do you care?"

"Right," I said. "I shouldn't care. It doesn't matter."

Except it did matter. I couldn't get it out of my mind that everything about Lance felt calculated—his transformation, his tragic backstory, his knowledge about my family, his subtle flirtations, his even more subtle invasion of my personal space.

There's something off about him. I know it.

But saying that aloud would make me sound as delusional as Mom thought I was.

Besides, he was almost done with his work in the house. The water mitigation stuff would be done tomorrow, and he could repair the toilet, tile, and do the painting in a day or so, according to him. I could manage to endure him until his time here wound down.

After that, I never had to see him again.

13: JESSICA

The next morning, Sunday, Lance texted at exactly eleven o'clock.

Good morning. I'd like to visit in thirty minutes to gauge progress. Is that acceptable, ma'am?

I glared at my phone. With his exaggerated formality, he was still mocking me.

It's acceptable, I replied.

He sent back a salute emoji. I rolled my eyes.

"Lance is on the way," I told Mom. She sat on the deck again, reading her dog-eared Bible, coffee at her side. After another long night of the droning equipment, neither of us had mustered the energy for church—honestly, my attendance had always been sporadic at best—but Mom's Sunday morning scripture reading served as her private worship in lieu of a church visit.

"Let's pray he takes away those horrible machines," she said. "I can't handle much more."

"I want all of this to be over," I said.

Lance arrived in exactly thirty minutes. He had an almost mechanical sense of timeliness, I'd noticed.

I opened the door before he could knock.

"There you are." He flashed a warm smile. "You look fresh and lovely this morning, Jessica."

"Did you sneak into my bedroom yesterday?"

I'd decided to ambush him with the question immediately—no preamble, no warning—to observe his unguarded reaction.

"I did not." His expression remained perfectly neutral. "I would never violate a client's personal space. Did something happen?"

He was either the best liar I'd ever seen—and I'd seen some masters of the game—or I was manufacturing threats from nothing.

His gaze held mine with unwavering sincerity. No shifting eyes, no defensive body language, no telltale micro expressions. Either he possessed sociopathic-level control over his reactions, or he was telling the truth.

But my underwear drawer hadn't rearranged itself.

"Someone moved my clothes in a drawer," I said, watching his chiseled face. "Private clothes."

"That's concerning." His brow furrowed. "Have you considered that your mother might have been tidying your room? Sometimes family members help with laundry or organization without mentioning it—or they forget. Has Mrs. Taylor been dealing with any memory issues lately?"

I hesitated. Mom did occasionally "help" with tasks I hadn't requested, her frequent memory gaps making her forget she'd done them.

"Maybe," I said. "She has good days and bad days, I guess."

"I take professional boundaries very seriously, Jessica." His voice carried wounded dignity. "My reputation depends on trust. If you're uncomfortable with me working here, I can recommend another contractor from HandyHelper."

"Let's just check the moisture levels," I said. "We're close to getting this done, hopefully."

"Of course." His smile returned, warm and forgiving. "I understand you're under tremendous stress—the divorce, the business launch, moving back home, trying to help out your mother. Stress can make us see threats where none exist."

"Forget about it," I said. I made an awkward waving gesture. "Do your thing, please."

"Five minutes," he said.

I'd planned on asking him about Melody Rockwell, but worried bringing that up might make me sound even more delusional—or plain callous. What would any reasonable person think if someone revealed they were digging into the fate of your late spouse?

I didn't need to follow him around the house, either. I'd already closed—and locked—my bedroom door. I sat on the sofa in the family room, clasping my phone in my lap, hoping for good news so we could get back to our lives.

One by one, I heard the fans and dehumidifiers fall silent at last, first in the kitchen, and then, upstairs. The pressure on my ears eased.

I rose as Lance came downstairs, his footfalls thundering on the staircase. He clicked his tongue and gave me a thumbs-up.

"We're good?" I asked.

"Mitigation complete."

"Thank goodness."

"I know this experience has been disruptive. If it's acceptable to you, I can start on the restoration work immediately: tile, new toilet, painting the kitchen ceiling."

"How long will it take?"

"If I start now, I can complete the project in about seven hours. I'll be out of here in time for Sunday dinner."

"You have everything you need to get started? Today? Matching paint and tile for the bathroom?"

"I expected you'd want to wrap this job today. I planned ahead." He flashed another disarming smile.

"You're good at your job. I'll grant you that." *Even though I still don't trust you.*

"I'm good at a lot of different things," he said, and I caught a flirtatious note. He followed with: "But I'm especially skilled at my profession."

"If we can close this out today, I'm all for it. Please wrap it up."

"Yes, ma'am." He gave me a theatrical salute, but at that point, I didn't care. I wanted him gone—the sooner, the better.

Mom wandered inside then, and naturally, she swooned at his attention as he chatted her up and started the restoration work. I decided to hunker down in my bedroom to do my own work. The disruptions over the past few days had put me behind, and I needed to get back on track for the upcoming week.

When I emerged from my room a couple of hours later to refresh my water bottle, I checked in the bathroom across the hallway and discovered he had already removed the old toilet and installed the replacement tiles. A new one stood on a tarp, awaiting installation.

Wow, this guy is a machine, I thought. Despite myself, I was impressed.

Downstairs, the distinctive smell of fresh paint filled the air. Lance had started painting the kitchen ceiling, using broad, smooth brushstrokes. Plastic sheets had been draped over much of the kitchen to protect the floor, countertops, and appliances from dripping paint.

Yet Mom stood nearby, cupping a coffee mug in her slender hands. Both of them laughed at something as I came inside, as if sharing a private joke, but when I glanced at Mom, she looked away from me and ran her hand through her hair, a nervous gesture I recognized.

What's going on here?

"Is everything okay?" I asked.

"Of course," Mom said. "We're only catching up on local gossip. Lance here has worked for half of the town, it seems."

Lance said nothing, only continued his brushstrokes. I wasn't sure I believed Mom—she had never been a convincing liar—but I wasn't going to press the issue in front of him. If what she'd said was only half-true I didn't need Lance adding us to his "local gossip" talk.

After working for a bit longer, I ran an errand—first making sure I locked my bedroom door—to the supermarket to pick up items for dinner. When I returned, I didn't see either Lance or Mom in the kitchen, so I assumed he was installing the toilet.

As I loaded groceries into the refrigerator and cabinets, I heard Lance's footsteps approach.

"Sunday dinner on the way, hmm?" he asked, eyebrows arched.

"I'll wait until you leave to get started," I said.

"What's on the menu tonight?"

"Chili."

"Ah. I love a nice, hearty bowl of chili on a cool October evening."

"It reminds me of my dad," I said. "He made the best chili ever but he'd only do it during football season."

"He was a good man. I'm sure you miss him."

I smiled, thinking of Dad.

"I'll be done soon," Lance said. "No pressure, but I was thinking —we should get together some time soon. I'd love to take you to dinner."

Here we go, I thought. I should have expected this. Although Lance was an incredibly handsome man, I wasn't twenty-two anymore, when all it took for me to say yes to a date was sweet talk and a charming smile—I was a battle-hardened forty-three-year-old and had learned to trust my instincts. Lance had so many red flags that every fiber of my being screamed, *No way.*

"Thank you for the offer, but that's not a good idea. My divorce was finalized only a week ago, Lance."

He stared at me, expressionless.

"It's not a good time," I said. And it would *never* be a good time.

He continued to look at me, silent. I couldn't endure that strange, unblinking stare. I flicked hair away from my face and turned back to the refrigerator, even though I'd already put away groceries.

The silence stretched on.

"You said you're almost done?" I asked, just to break the eerie quiet. "What's left for you to do? I'd like to get dinner started soon for me and Mom."

"There's the matter of the invoice," he said in a flat tone.

"Mom's homeowner's insurance is going to cover it. Email the final invoice to me, please. I'm working with the claim adjustor. I'll make sure you get paid this week even if I have to pay you myself."

"Then we're about done here. I'll clean up, do my final checks, and be on my way. I'll be looking for your five-star review on Handy-Helper, Jessica. Can I count on you for that?"

Without waiting for my reply, he walked out.

14: JESSICA

With Lance's restoration work done and order restored in the house, at last, I fell back into a productive groove the following week: holding Zoom calls with prospects and conducting in-person sales presentations at local businesses, all of which went extremely well and netted me more contracts for media campaigns.

I had to land several more deals to replace my prior salary, but I was confident that I could pull it off. I had the wind at my back.

That Friday, I left home in the morning for another face-to-face presentation, at a restaurant in downtown Newnan. Afterward, I met a college student, a potential intern, for lunch. I needed someone to assist with setting up and managing the campaigns, and a cheap but eager intern was the perfect candidate. I'd done the same thing myself back in my younger days.

Around one, I pulled into our driveway—and braked hard, my heart lurching into my throat.

"No," I said aloud.

Lance's black Mercedes-Benz cargo van was parked in the driveway, the rear of the vehicle facing the house. As if he was here for a job, not a social call.

What was he doing here? We'd paid his invoice in full yesterday. I'd even posted a five-star review of his work on the app, keeping my comments brief but positive. What was left? What did he want?

He'd arranged his van at an angle that blocked me from parking behind Mom's Camry. I had to walk a greater distance to get to the house, my work bag swinging from my shoulder, my hands clenched into fists.

Inside, I saw Lance in the living room. He stood on a ladder and worked on installing what looked like a new ceiling fan; an opened box lay nearby.

"Hey there, Jessica." He waved, screwdriver in hand.

"What are you doing here?"

"Installing a new fan. The old one was broken. Hadn't you noticed?"

My head felt as if it were being squeezed in an iron vise. "Where my mother?"

"She's lounging on the back deck. I'll be working on the deck, as well—so *many* repairs and improvements needed here. I'm going to be busy for quite some time with you two ladies."

No, no, no.

I spun away from him and marched toward the kitchen, to the patio door. Mom was coming inside as I approached.

"What is Lance doing here, Mom? Did you hire him?"

Mom straightened. "The house needs a lot of work, Jessie. Isn't that obvious?"

"Why didn't you talk to me about it first?"

"It's still my house, remember?" She softened her blunt words with a smile. "Lance is offering us the family discount, again. He's wonderful." Mom strolled to the counter and selected a new tea bag from a tray. "He reminds me of that sweet boy who mowed our lawn when your father was recovering from back surgery. What was his name? Larry?"

"Mom, that's *Lance*. The same guy standing in our living room."

Mom laughed, waved off her memory lapse. "Of course it is. It's going to be so nice having him here for a while to repair this old, crumbling house. He can fix anything, sweetheart."

"How long?" I asked.

"He's created a rather lengthy list of projects and I agree with them all. Several weeks, perhaps?" Mom patted my arm. "I gave him a spare key, so he can come and go as he pleases."

"You gave him a spare key." I felt numb.

"Of course. It will be easier for everyone that way, don't you agree?"

From the kitchen, I heard heavy footsteps creaking up the staircase and then thudding along the second-floor hallway. I hadn't locked my door. Was he invading my room again already?

How was I going to live like this?

15: JESSICA

I caught Lance when he was halfway down the driveway, his toolbox swinging at his side as he headed toward his van. The afternoon sun glinted off its black paint, and I squinted against the glare as I descended the creaky veranda steps.

"I know what you're up to here," I said.

He had already installed the new ceiling fan in the living room that afternoon, but I knew of his "rather lengthy list" of projects, as Mom had said, that could keep him here for weeks—months, maybe.

I couldn't stand there and let it happen.

At my words, Lance stopped in mid-step, his broad shoulders going still before he slowly turned to face me. That practiced smile was already in place, but I was done being polite.

"You went behind my back to make a deal with my mother," I said. My voice came out sharper than I'd intended, but I didn't soften it. "So you can work here ongoing and try to wear me down."

Lance set down his toolbox on the back of Mom's car with deliberate care, then straightened to his full height. He was at least six or seven inches taller than me, a mountain of a man.

"Wear you down," he repeated. "That's an interesting way to characterize my professional services, Jessica."

"Don't play games with me." I balled my hands into fists on my waist. "I'm not going to change my mind about going out with you, so let's end this charade. I'll pay you for the work you did today, and then we're done for good."

His smile flickered—on, off, on—like a faulty light bulb struggling against a bad connection. The effect was unsettling, as if something behind his pleasant facade had short-circuited.

"Your mother is the homeowner . . . Jessica." He said my name like he was savoring the sound of it, tasting each syllable. "Marilyn Taylor is printed on the release of lien."

His comment was like a jab to my gut. He had reviewed the release of lien? I hadn't even seen that document myself, but I knew what it signified: Mom's full ownership of the property, free of any bank loan.

"When did you—" I started, then stopped. "How do you have access to that?"

His smile brightened and I realized something about him then: He *enjoyed* making me uncomfortable.

"Public county records," he said. "Your mother mentioned she was considering refinancing, and she asked my opinion on whether the improvements would add value." He tilted his head, studying my reaction. "I did my due diligence. It's part of providing comprehensive service to my clients, especially those who have highly valuable properties."

"My mother's not making the best decisions right now," I said, struggling to keep my voice steady. "I know you've noticed—"

"She allowed her firstborn, forty-three-year-old child to move back home." Lance took a step closer, and I had to resist the urge to backpedal to the veranda steps. "Was that a poor decision? Should mommy have refused to let you limp back into the nest after your marriage imploded and you got fired from your job?"

My throat tightened. How did he know about my job? I'd never mentioned being laid off. Had Mom told him? How much of my business was she telling this guy?

"I didn't get *fired*," I said, wondering why I felt the need to clarify that point with someone like him. "It was a layoff. Not that any of it is your business."

"You're here again only due to your mother's kindness, but in case you missed the memo: Mom's house. Mom's rules."

"Listen, this isn't about—"

"If you can't tolerate me being here," he interrupted, "perhaps *you* should leave. Not having you around would make my job much easier, actually. Your mother and I work well together. She appreciates a man who can take care of things."

His words took root in my brain, and suddenly I saw it all with awful clarity: Lance wasn't here for me at all. He wasn't trying to ignite some romance that had never sparked in high school.

He was here for Mom.

Or, more specifically, for what Mom represented: A lonely widow, financially vulnerable, isolated from family, living in a mortgage-free house that was probably worth close to half a million dollars despite its condition. An aging woman whose memory was crumbling, who craved male attention and validation, who'd been primed by years of widowhood to welcome a helpful, charming man into her life—someone she already trusted from prior history and family connections.

He's from a good family . . .

I was only an inconvenient complication who saw through his facade.

"This isn't about me at all, is it?" I said, not expecting him to tell me the truth. "You're planning something, aren't you? Some kind of dirty, long con job. You know this house is worth a fortune."

Lance's smile never wavered, but something altered in his eyes. I saw an icy flatness that hadn't been there before, like a shark's gaze.

"Those are serious accusations, Jessica. Slanderous, in fact." His tone remained conversational. "I'm a licensed contractor with a pristine reputation. Over two hundred five-star reviews on Handy-Helper, as you saw yourself. Everyone in town knows me, loves me. Ask yourself: Who sounds more credible? An upstanding business owner like me, or a bitter, unemployed divorcée who's acted unstable since moving back home with her mother?"

"Unstable? What?"

"Your mother's mentioned your mood swings. How you've been acting paranoid since your messy divorce from your unfaithful ex. Seeing threats where none exist." He shook his head with what looked like genuine sympathy. "Moving your own underwear and then accusing others of violating your privacy. It's troubling behavior, really. The kind of thing that makes people wonder if someone's experiencing a nervous breakdown, a midlife crisis, maybe."

I felt myself trembling. "You were in my room. I *know* you were."

"But you can't prove it, can you? And your mother will support that you've been under tremendous stress from the broken marriage, the lost job, the struggle to build a business. Probably not thinking rationally. Making fanciful accusations against someone who's only trying to help a sweet, deserving widow."

I didn't know what to say. The systematic way he'd built himself up, undermined my credibility, coaxed Mom to buy into it—it was genius. Chilling, but genius.

It was his plan all along, but you invited him in, Jess. You're the one who opened the door for the wolf.

"But if you choose to stick around?" He picked up his toolbox again, his smile brightening. "We'll have to learn to coexist. You'll see that I'm a great guy. Your mother already knows it. Everyone can see it except you."

"I'm the only one who has her eyes open," I said.

"Give me a chance, hmm?" He cocked his head again, and I realized it was a calculated gesture, probably practiced in a mirror. Everything about him was orchestrated. "Stop fighting the inevitable. Your mother wants me here. Why can't you just be happy for her?"

Something in my chest tightened into a cold, hard knot.

"I'm going to get you out of this house if it's the last thing I do," I said. "That's a promise."

For a heartbeat, his mask slipped. His expression went blank, and I saw the real Lance underneath—patient, predatory, utterly frightening.

Then the smile returned, brighter than ever.

"We'll see," he said.

He turned away, dismissing me as if I'd ceased to exist. His whistle started before he'd taken three steps—high and clear and cheerful. It took me a moment to recognize the tune: "Girls Just Want to Have Fun."

He was *mocking* me. Again. From the start, he'd never considered me a serious obstacle to whatever plan he was executing.

Behind me, I heard the front door rattle open.

"Jessie?" It was Mom, bright and innocent. "Is everything all right out here?"

Before I could answer, Mom shifted her attention to Lance.

"Lance, will you be staying for dinner, honey? I'm making my famous seafood gumbo."

Lance glanced back at me over his shoulder, and his smile said everything: *I've already won.*

"I'd love to, Mrs. Taylor, but I've got to go visit Pops at the assisting living center," he said. "I promised to bring him dinner. He doesn't ask for much these days, but he loves Burger King."

"How about if I pack some gumbo for you to take with you?" Mom said. "It would be far more nourishing than a greasy cheeseburger."

"That sounds wonderful, ma'am," he said.

Mom glanced at me before she ducked back inside, her eyes bright with excitement.

But a fresh chill slid down my spine, and I knew the first thing I had to do, today.

Put a new lock on my bedroom door.

16: JESSICA

"Let me make sure I understand this, Sis," Junior said, his voice crackling slightly through the FaceTime connection. "Mom gave some handyman the key to the house, and you think he's up to no good?"

It was early Friday evening, and I'd called Junior while sitting in my car parked in the driveway. Lance had left the house maybe two hours ago, toting a sealed plastic container of Mom's renowned gumbo—the good Tupperware, I'd noticed, the kind she usually reserved for church potlucks. He'd practically leered at me as he got in his van, triumphant in his new role.

Tomorrow, he would be back for another "job." I'd overheard him discussing it with Mom.

Out of desperation, I'd reached out to my brother, Lawrence Junior. Mom might brush off my warnings about Lance—and she had, repeatedly, with that infuriating patience she used when she thought I was being irrational. But she would listen to Junior. She *always* listened to Junior.

Junior was everything that I was not: a man, happily married, a parent to Mom's adorable grandchildren, and successful in his career.

The golden child who'd never stumbled, never divorced, never had to crawl back home at forty-three with nothing but a car full of boxes and a bruised ego.

Junior was forty, three years younger than me. We hadn't been close since we were younger children, our paths diverging when I hit my teens and become obsessed with boys and socializing, while Junior focused on athletics, eventually earning a college scholarship to play baseball. I usually only saw him around the holidays, when he brought his family from Chicago back down to Georgia, and we chatted just a few times a year—polite, surface-level conversations that never went much deeper than weather, work, and generic family news.

I'd texted him first and convinced him to join me on a FaceTime call, hinting obliquely that "it's about Mom," and launching into a brief explanation as soon as the call started, before he could interrupt me.

Junior and my late father looked so much alike that it was eerie, especially now that Junior was fighting a receding hairline. Same broad forehead, same deep-set eyes, same way of pursing his lips when he was about to disagree with you. Seeing him on the screen felt like looking at a ghost of Dad's younger self.

"His name is Lance Cutler," I said. "He was a year ahead of me in school, and apparently he did some yardwork for us a long time ago, when Dad had his back surgery. Now he's a handyman here in town."

"Never heard of him," Junior said. His tone was already dismissive, that lawyer voice he used when he'd concluded something wasn't worth his time.

"Well, I'm telling you about him." Cold perspiration prickled my forehead, and I struggled to keep my voice calm. "He's good at his job, but I think he's scheming to take advantage of Mom, financially. Like I said, she's given him a key to the house and he's basically here indefinitely."

"The house needs a ton of work, Sis." Junior shifted on-screen, and I could see he was in his kitchen, the quartzite countertops and high-end appliances gleaming behind him. "You surely see that now that you moved back home."

"I'm not denying that, but—"

"Do you have any evidence of what he's 'scheming,' as you call it?" He used one hand to put air quotes around the word *scheming,* his platinum wedding band catching the light.

My jaw clenched. I should have expected this line of questioning from Junior. He was a courtroom defense attorney, after all, accustomed to protecting rich scumbag clients from prosecutors. Everything was evidence and burden of proof with him. Nothing could just *feel* wrong.

"He's already checked into the release of lien," I said. "He told me that himself. He knows that Mom owns the house free and clear."

"You've concluded that because this Lance character knows a little about Mom's financial situation—based on public records, I might add—that he's suddenly a con artist?" Junior gave me a skeptical look. "That sounds a tad bit circumstantial, Sis."

Circumstantial. The word felt like a slap.

"Stop the lawyer mumbo-jumbo, will you? I'm worried about Mom, okay? This guy is bad news, I know it, and I want *you* to ask *her* to make him leave."

"One sec." Junior frowned at me, his tapered eyebrows drawing together the same way Dad's used to, and then he put the phone down. The screen showed me a view of his kitchen ceiling—heavenly white paint, a modern pendant light fixture. Top-dollar stuff.

I heard his voice, muffled and distant, talking to one of his little kids. He made some comment about "Auntie Jessie" that I struggled to catch. Someone giggled—probably Layla, his daughter. The sound was bright and carefree, so different from the tension in my own chest.

Then Layla plucked the phone from wherever Junior had set it and gave me a gap-toothed grin—she was all of five years old and truly adorable.

"Hey, Auntie Jessie," she said, her face filling the screen.

Sighing, I switched on a smile, though it felt like a mask sliding into place. "Hi, sweetie. How are you?"

"Good," she said, her eyes glittering with the innocent happiness of childhood. "Are you working now?"

"I'm off work, baby. Can you give the phone back to your daddy, please?"

"Daddy went to the potty." She giggled as if this were the funniest thing ever. "He said he'll call you back."

"Okay," I said, my smile starting to hurt. "Well, I love you all. I'll see you soon, okay?"

"Love you, too!" Layla sang, and then the screen went black.

I stared at my reflection in the darkened phone display. My eyes looked as hollow as I felt.

Fifteen minutes later, Junior still hadn't called me back.

That sounds a tad bit circumstantial, Sis...

He thought I was paranoid, I realized. He didn't understand the need to take action, to warn Mom that she had opened the door to trouble by hiring Lance long-term and giving him his own key. To Junior, safely swaddled in his perfect life up in Chicago, this was probably just a case of his dramatic older sister overreacting. Probably thought I was cracking up after the divorce—I could only imagine what Mom might have told him.

That left me as the only one who could see the threat Lance represented.

Still, I tried calling Junior again. When he didn't answer, I followed up with a text: *We weren't finished talking. Call me back.*

Five minutes later, he responded: *Sorry, busy with the kiddos. Honestly not sure this is a real issue with Mom that needs my involvement, Sis. Mom can handle her own business. She's sharp as a whip. See you at Thanksgiving.*

"Why did I even bother?" I muttered to myself.

I racked the phone in the dashboard mount with more force than necessary, the plastic rattling. I leaned my head back against the seat, closing my eyes against the late afternoon sun slanting through the windshield.

You're on your own with this one, Jessie, I thought.

I opened my eyes and stared at the house. Somewhere inside, Mom was probably puttering around the kitchen or in her garden, singing to herself, oblivious to the danger I could feel building in my bones like a brewing storm.

I would have to handle this myself.

Somehow.

17: MARILYN

The tension between me and Jessica felt thick enough to choke on.

Over the years, I'd weathered countless storms with Jessica, my eldest child, my difficult daughter. She had firm opinions about everything—politics, religion, work, how I folded towels or used too much butter when cooking, how I made too much noise during her business calls. Strong-willed, like her father. Larry had that same way of setting his jaw when he'd made up his mind about something, that same hot flash of defiance in his eyes.

But I was never one to back down from a healthy debate, either. Perhaps she'd inherited that quality from me and not Larry after all. We were more alike than she'd ever admit.

This disagreement over Lance, though—this felt different. It lay heavy on my shoulders, like a winter coat. Why couldn't she understand that I only wanted stability? A comfortable house for the two of us? Someone trustworthy and knowledgeable to lend assistance?

After I'd sent Lance home that afternoon with a Tupperware container of seafood gumbo—still warm, the spices perfuming the entire downstairs—Jessica had stormed outside without a word. Just that tight-lipped fury, her jaw clenched in a way that reminded me too much of myself. I'd watched her from behind the living room curtain.

She got inside her car in a huff. She sat in it for over half an hour, talking and gesturing with angry movements that made my stomach twist. Without hearing a word, I knew she was discussing our disagreement with someone on the phone.

Afterward, she peeled out of the driveway and drove off—and returned an hour later with plastic bags from The Home Depot. She barely glanced at me as she marched to the staircase.

"What's that?" I asked from the living room sofa, which was so much more comfortable now that we had a functional ceiling fan overhead to distribute cool air.

"Privacy." She pounded up the steps.

I followed, my hand trailing along the banister Lance had tightened during a prior visit. No more wobbling. Things in this house were coming together again.

In the hallway outside her bedroom, Jessica knelt on the carpet, pulling items from her bags with aggressive efficiency. A small toolbox, and a silver doorknob that caught the hallway light, metal gleaming.

"You're installing a new lock?" I asked.

"I'm making sure I have privacy." She cut open the package. "Since you've decided to invite a stranger to come inside the house whenever he feels like it."

I felt my spine stiffen.

"Lance isn't a stranger. We know his family. Don't you remember his mother from the restaurant in town? She was a sweet lady, always had a lovely smile for everyone."

Jessica finally wrestled open the package and extracted a small screwdriver from the toolbox. She attacked the existing doorknob with it, jamming the tip into the screw head at an awkward angle. The screwdriver slipped, gouging a line in the wood.

"You're going to damage the door," I said.

She ignored me, continuing her clumsy assault on the hardware. A small vein pulsed at her temple, her lips tight with concentration.

"I'd like a key for this new lock of yours," I said.

A laugh escaped her, but she glared at me with such intensity that I took an involuntary step backward.

"So you can give it to Lance? I'm sorry, Mom, but I can't do that."

"There could be an emergency when you're not here—"

"No, Mom."

I hesitated, feeling the ground shift beneath my feet. "It's my house, Jessie. My rules."

Her hands stilled on the doorknob. She turned to look at me fully, and something in her expression made my stomach plummet.

"Did *he* tell you to say that to me?" she said.

The question landed like an accusation. Had I discussed owner-ship with Lance? Property rights? Jessica's place in my home? He had such strong opinions about so many things—about boundaries, about respect, about how children should treat their parents. The conversations blurred together in my mind.

"I've got to insist upon having a key." But even as the words left my mouth, I heard the weakness in them. My voice wavered, thin as crepe paper. I couldn't force my daughter to give me a key, could I? She was a grown woman, not a child anymore.

Jessica returned to her awkward installation attempt, the screw-driver slipping again, this time with enough force that her knuckles scraped against the metal plate.

I forced a chuckle, though it sounded hollow in the hallway. "Lance could no doubt complete this installation in fifteen minutes. It's going to take you hours, if you manage it at all."

Her glare could have liquefied steel.

"He could also replace it—at my request," I said, my voice hardening.

"If he takes it off, I'll put it right back on," she said. "If you want to play that game, Mom, go right ahead."

She had an answer for everything, didn't she? Just like when she was a teenager, always so quick with a retort, always needing the last word. I'd admired that quality once—her gumption, her fire. *With this attitude, my girl will go far in life*, I used to think.

Now it just felt exhausting.

"I'll *allow* you to install this lock, for now, Jessie." I squared my shoulders, trying to reclaim some authority. "But this is immature behavior, to be frank. You're acting as if you're sixteen again with secrets to hide."

"There's no secrets, Mom. I don't want your wonderful Lance pawing through my panties again and pretending that I'm imagining things."

Pawing through her panties? Why was she still insisting that violation had occurred? Lance had even mentioned her accusation to me—Jessie had confronted the man with her claims—and he'd appeared deeply wounded. Clearly, she had misplaced her own personal items, but in her rush to judgment she was alienating a decent man who wanted only to help us.

Just like her husband—pardon me, *ex*-husband. Mitch was a fine man. I obviously didn't condone adultery, but had my daughter bothered to get marital counseling? Did she talk to their pastor? How much effort did she invest in saving her marriage?

She'd brought that same bitterness to her perceptions of Lance. She might have ruined her own life, but I wouldn't allow her to ruin this opportunity for me to restore my home.

"I'm not going to exhaust myself arguing with you about these things any longer," I said. "I'll be downstairs."

"Good."

Inwardly, I winced at her tone.

I didn't see Jessica for the remainder of the evening. Didn't hear her come down for a snack or a drink. Didn't hear anything but the occasional muffled thump from upstairs as she toiled away on her ridiculous lock.

The tension sat in my stomach like a sour, undigested meal, and I tried to push it away.

She'll come around eventually, I thought. I was her mother. I knew what was best for both of us.

In the end, I was always right.

18: JESSICA

First things first: I needed to learn a lot more about Lance Cutler. I had to gather hard, irrefutable evidence of his ulterior motives. Not gut feelings.

Junior's dismissive remark from yesterday still stung: *A tad bit circumstantial, Sis.*

But if I couldn't convince my brother that anything was amiss, Mom would be even harder to win over. Only cold facts would open her eyes to the threat that Lance presented.

I kicked off Saturday with an early morning workout at the high school track, came back home, showered, made coffee, and locked myself in my bedroom. Through the window, I could see Mom already in her garden, kneeling beside her plants in the morning sun. Her gray hair caught the light, turning it silver. She wore those ratty blue gardening gloves with the torn thumb, the ones she refused to replace.

We hadn't spoken to each other since yesterday's confrontation. If she was waiting for me to apologize, she would be waiting a long time.

Sitting at my desk, a steaming mug of coffee at my elbow and my laptop open in front of me, I started my investigation at the source: HandyHelper.

The company behind the software offered a desktop version of the app. I opened a web browser, logged into my account, and accessed my history, where I found my recent interactions with "Lance C."

My five-star review made me grimace.

"Lance responded immediately to our plumbing emergency and fixed the problem efficiently and professionally. Highly recommend."

Why had I felt pressured to rate him so highly despite my misgivings? Trying to be "nice," maybe?

The app didn't allow me to amend my review, and anyway, changing my rating wasn't my objective: I needed to scrutinize what other clients had said about him.

At the time I'd hired him—water pouring through the kitchen ceiling, Mom in hysterics, disaster breathing down our necks—I hadn't examined his profile closely. I'd seen the overall ranking, skimmed maybe three reviews, read his generic bio with that vague sense of familiarity, and clicked "Message" in desperation.

That was behind me now. I needed to do a deep dive on this guy.

Lance's overall rating was 4.8 stars, out of 223 reviews. The ratings breakdown overwhelmingly showed five-star reviews; a sprinkling of four-stars, and one—literally just *one*—one-star rating.

Clients were identified only by first name and last initial. No photos, no additional information, no way to contact them. My review as "Jessica T." was the most recent one.

Virtually *all* the reviewers were women:

Barbara J.

Susan B.

Patricia W.

Dorothy L.

Linda P.

The names suggested middle age and older. Women who owned homes, women who probably lived alone. The pattern was obvious now that I was looking for it, glaring at me from the screen.

Coincidence? I doubted that. It was strategic.

If my name had been *Zoey T.*, twenty-two years old and living in a condo downtown, he probably wouldn't have answered my message at all. I was useful only as an entry point to Mom. He'd tried to butter me up, too, from the little compliments to asking me to dinner. If I'd accepted the invite, I was convinced he would have just strung me along to keep me on his side and out of the way.

I kept scrolling. Every review came with a reply from him— warm, friendly, attentive. *"It was a pleasure to serve you!"* or *"Thank you for trusting me with your home!"* Always personal, like he remembered each client intimately.

Near the bottom, I finally located that lone one-star rating, from "Evelyn A." the previous April.

"Lance did a great job installing new tile in the master bath at a fair price, but after the work was done, he kept calling me to offer additional service. I'm on a fixed income and can't afford all these extra projects he says I needed. I had to block his phone number."

Now, this was interesting—and seemed familiar. It was exactly what he was doing to us. The endless list of "necessary" repairs. The pressure, subtle but relentless, to let him deeper into our lives, deeper into our home.

Naturally, Lance responded to this unflattering feedback.

"I'm grateful for the opportunity to repair your bathroom tile and pleased you were happy with the work. During the job, you mentioned other improvements you'd like to make, and I followed up only twice to get details. I regret if you felt this was too persistent. I strive to provide excellent service to all my clients within their budget."

He'd turned it around. *You mentioned other improvements . . .* A polite gaslighting, wrapped in customer-service language. Deflecting responsibility, making it her idea. Minimizing his behavior—*only twice*, as if that made it acceptable. The classic non-apology: *I regret if you felt this was too persistent . . .*

I stared at the screen. I couldn't contact Evelyn; the app protected her anonymity. But I could picture her—a woman living alone, charmed at first by his good looks and professionalism, and then turned off by his oily persistence and forced to block his number.

Had Lance assessed her property's value, too? Calculated her net worth? Tried to get a key?

And what about the ones who'd given him that key? What had happened to them?

I chewed on my bottom lip, picked up my coffee, and found it had turned cold.

Unfortunately, this wasn't the quality of proof that I could present to Mom. She would scoff at this reviewer, Evelyn A., and take Lance's side.

HandyHelper wasn't going to help me this time. I'd have to find evidence somewhere else.

Time to dig deeper.

19: JESSICA

I went downstairs into the kitchen to refresh my coffee, my bare feet cold against the tile. The pot was still hot, steam rising from the carafe in lazy spirals. I was reaching for the handle when I heard the back door open.

Mom came inside from the garden, dirt smudged on her gloves, the scent of raw soil following her into the kitchen. We both froze for a half-second, our first time occupying the same space since yesterday's argument.

"Hello, Jessica," Mom said, her tone stiff as her upper lip. She pulled off her gloves with sharp movements.

"Good morning, Mother." I could be formal, too. I poured coffee into my mug, the dark liquid streaming out with a sound that seemed too loud in the silence.

Her nose wrinkled as she studied me. "I saw you leave earlier. Did you already exercise?"

"I put in my five thousand steps at the track."

She gave me a once-over and a slight nod, as if grading my performance. "You just might stick to this."

"I just might." I sipped my coffee. "I'm very focused when I set my mind on something. Iron-willed."

"Hmph. So I've learned over the years."

Tight-lipped, she shuffled out of the kitchen, but we'd broken the silence between us. An uneasy detente, maybe. I knew Mom wouldn't apologize for what she'd said, and neither would I—because I had meant every word.

Back in my room, I sat in front of my laptop again and expanded my investigation into Lance Cutler beyond HandyHelper, by typing "Lance + Cutler + Handyman" into Google.

The first search result? His contractor profile on HandyHelper, which I'd already dissected. Nothing new there.

I scrolled down. Nothing else matched what I was looking for.

My jaw clenched.

I kept digging. Tried Facebook. Instagram. LinkedIn. Twitter. Nextdoor. TikTok. I searched Yelp, Thumbtack, Angi. Checked business directories.

Nothing. Lance Cutler didn't exist in any of the usual places.

No Facebook page with smiling photos and customer testimonials. No LinkedIn profile boasting about his skills and experience. No business website with a portfolio of completed projects. Not even a sparse Instagram account with before-and-after shots.

He was only on HandyHelper.

I leaned back in my chair, the springs creaking beneath me. Sipping coffee, I frowned at the screen.

His relative lack of online presence was strange, wasn't it? More than strange. It felt deliberate. Calculated.

In today's world, everyone had a digital footprint. Especially someone running a business. Heck, my great-aunt Ruby owned a Facebook profile up until the time of her passing a few years back at the age of ninety-five, even if she'd only used it to repost cake recipes and photos of her grandchildren.

But Lance? Nothing.

HandyHelper might have been the only source of leads he

needed. Between that and perhaps word of mouth, he could have an endless supply of projects. Older women recommending him to their friends, creating a network of trusting clients.

But that didn't feel right to me.

A legitimate business *wanted* to be known far and wide. My own freelance marketing consultant enterprise was built entirely on expanding companies' digital footprints, on being findable, on cultivating an online presence that promoted credibility and professionalism.

But it seemed as if Lance wanted to minimize his.

The question was: Why?

I drummed my fingers against the desk.

Keep digging.

I found the Better Business Bureau website for Georgia, typed "Lance Cutler" and "Newnan" into their contractor search engine.

A result popped up. He was listed—with a BBB rating of "A+."

But as I read the page, my brief flicker of hope died. The listing provided only the most basic information imaginable: name, phone number, city. No street address. No business description. No website link. The BBB file had been opened over ten years ago, which suggested legitimacy—except for how sparse the information was.

He had eight reviews, all of them glowing.

I recognized the names immediately: Dorothy L., Linda P., Patricia W.—the same women from his HandyHelper profile. The same pattern of older female clients leaving the same kind of effusive praise.

"Lance is a godsend!"

"So reliable and trustworthy!"

"I don't know what I'd do without him!"

The BBB portal didn't provide any additional data on the customers. There was no way to contact them. No way to verify if these women were real, or if something had happened to them after they'd left these reviews.

No one had posted a complaint, either. Not one.

I shook my head, pressure building behind my eyes. None of this was helping me. Every avenue I pursued led to the same carefully curated image: Lance Cutler, reliable handyman with impeccable ratings and virtually no verifiable existence outside a single app and a sparse BBB listing.

A troubling thought struck me: What if I was wrong about Lance?

What if he was only a simple local handyman with occasionally creepy tendencies? He focused on older women because they appreciated him, and he could easily persuade them to hire him for lucrative, ongoing work. That wasn't a crime. It could be just a savvy business model.

Maybe Mom was right, and I was overreacting. Paranoid. Seeing threats where there were none because my own life had fallen apart and I needed to pin blame on someone, anyone, for how I was feeling.

I cupped my hands around my coffee mug, stared at the laptop screen until my eyes blurred.

No. No, I wasn't wrong.

My instincts were screaming at me, and I'd ignored my instincts once before—with Mitch, with the signs I'd rationalized away until I couldn't anymore. I wouldn't make that mistake again.

I got up from my desk chair and paced the room, needing movement.

I was missing something. Approaching this from the wrong direction.

My gaze fell upon my high school yearbooks stacked on the dresser.

Melody Rockwell.

I needed to loop back to her, the high school sweetheart I'd assumed was "the love of my life" Lance had mentioned with such somber gravity. Lance hadn't been mentioned in her obituary ten years ago, and I had dropped it there, figured I was mistaken about their relationship.

I grabbed the yearbook I had marked with yellow Post-it notes and flipped to the candid shot of Lance and Melody, hugged up in front of the hallway lockers. I'd marked her class photo, too.

Yearbook in hand, I settled in front of my computer again and found Melody's obituary once more. The obit photo showed an older version of the girl from the yearbook, with something fragile in her smile.

The dates of her life were jarring: 1981–2015. Thirty-four years old. So young.

"She is survived by her parents, Robert and Margaret Rockwell, and her dear older sister, Ingrid . . ."

Although I had skimmed the obituary before, I read it again. And again.

No mention of Lance. Not a single reference to a husband, a spouse, a partner.

If they'd been married, why was his name omitted from her obituary? That was where surviving spouses were listed, where families acknowledged the people left behind.

Marriage records were kept in probate court. Mitch and I had married in Fulton County, gone through all the paperwork, the license, the filing.

Newnan was in Coweta County. If Lance and Melody had been married, it might have been recorded there.

I found the Georgia Probate Records website and typed "Rockwell, Melody" into the search fields.

The search wheel spun . . . and then, bingo.

Lance Cutler and Melody Rockwell had married in May 2012. The officiant was Charles Johnson, Pastor; the judge was Bernice Cranford.

Only three years after their wedding, Melody Rockwell—Melody Cutler?—had died.

Thirty-four years old. Three years of marriage. And an obituary that erased her husband's existence in her life.

Why?

I clicked back to the obituary, reading it again with fresh eyes. The language was careful, loving—describing Melody's kindness, her passion for nursing, her love of animals. Her family asked that donations be made to the animal shelter in her name rather than flowers.

But not a word about Lance.

They could have been divorced. Maybe it had been acrimonious —I knew a little about that kind of ending, the way love could curdle into something toxic that you wanted to forget forever. Maybe Melody's family had despised Lance and refused to acknowledge him even in her death.

I searched for divorce records. But unlike the marriage license, it turned out to be a more challenging task. The county required a formal request to be submitted via the superior court clerk's office, which meant forms, fees, processing time.

That would take too long. But there might be an easier way.

Would someone in Melody's family be willing to talk to me?

The thought churned my stomach. What would I even say? *Hey, you don't know me, but I'm investigating your dead daughter's ex-husband because my mom hired him and I think he's shady?*

But if there was information about Lance—about who he really was—her family would know.

Suddenly, I heard a door slam downstairs. Mom was talking to someone. I heard deep, resonant laughter.

Oh no, I thought with a sinking feeling.

I shot up from my chair and hurried to open my bedroom door so I could hear what this was all about.

I heard Mom's overly cheerful voice, clinking dishes, and more hearty laughter.

It was Lance, as I'd feared.

He was back already.

20: JESSICA

Why was Lance back again so soon?

I glanced at my phone—8:53 AM, on a Saturday morning. Way too early for a handyman visit. He'd been here just yesterday, for God's sake.

Although he was the subject of my research, I had no desire whatsoever to interact with him. It was important that he knew absolutely *nothing* about my investigation into his background. If I slipped up and shared something with him, or gave Mom a hint before I was fully prepared, I was convinced he would try to discredit me somehow. Spin some story to Mom. Make me sound paranoid and unstable. Like he'd done when I confronted him about moving my underwear.

Quietly, I closed my bedroom door again. I locked it, too, grateful I'd gone through the trouble of installing a new knob.

But after I'd drunk two cups of coffee and some water, my bladder had other plans. I pressed my ear to the door, listening. Footsteps in the kitchen. The faint clink of dishes. Mom's laughter.

Just go. Be quick.

I unlocked the door, hurried across the hallway into the bathroom. The new toilet—Lance's work—mocked me with its efficiency. I used it as quickly as possible, washed my hands and rinsed my face with cold water that did nothing to calm my thundering heart, and stepped back into the hallway—

—where Lance stood directly outside my bedroom door.

Not down the hallway. Not on the stairs. Right there, barely three feet away, as if he'd been waiting.

A strangled gasp escaped my throat before I could stop it.

His lips curved into that smile—the one that never reached his eyes. "Good morning, Jessica."

I felt heat dot my cheeks. The hallway suddenly felt too narrow. I could smell him—coffee and something sharp and astringent, like WD-40.

He was no longer wearing that alluring male fragrance. He had no need to woo me anymore.

"You're back already," I said.

"A handyman's work is never done." He pivoted to my door and tapped the new doorknob with the tip of his screwdriver. "New lock, hmm?"

"Security is important to me."

"I couldn't agree more, Jessica." That smile widened a fraction. "In fact, I'm installing a comprehensive security system in your mother's home today. Smart locks, for starters. Familiar with those?"

I frowned. "Mom asked for smart locks?"

He continued: "Then I'm putting in a control panel with cellular backup, motion-activated alarm sensors, exterior cameras covering every entrance. Living out here on the edge of town, with crime statistics being what they are . . ." He gestured vaguely, as if crime were something tangible lurking in every shadow. "You two ladies need to feel safe. Lucky for you I'm very knowledgeable about these things."

"There's plenty of other things you could be fixing here. I can't believe Mom asked you to install a security system."

"It's part of my Family Care Package."

"Family Care Package?"

"I take a holistic view of all aspects of the property." His tone shifted into something professorial, rehearsed. He gestured at the hallway, the walls, as if he could see through to the bones of the house. "Inside and out. Structure and security. Comfort and protection. What use is a renovated home without top-of-the-line monitoring to keep it all secure?" He tapped my doorknob again. "That's like driving a Bentley without door locks, hmm?"

"How much is my mother paying you for all this? She lives on a fixed income."

"Our financial arrangements are confidential, Jessica, but I can promise you, they're quite fair. I offer the best deal and the most comprehensive offerings on the market, for my select clients."

Select clients? What did that even mean?

"Was there a contract signed?" I asked. "If so, I want to see it."

"You'll have to speak to your mother about that, I'm afraid. It's not my practice to disclose contractual terms to anyone but the property owner. I'm sure you understand—professional boundaries and all that."

My shoulders tensed, muscles drawing taut across my back. He was going to keep throwing into my face the fact that I didn't have any ownership of the house, wasn't he? That I was only a guest here.

"As for this"—Lance turned back to the door and tapped the new lock with his screwdriver—"this isn't up to code."

"Not up to code?" I heard my voice rise to a shrill octave and fought to control it. "It's a doorknob!"

"Improper size and material specification for residential interior applications." He spoke with crisp certainty, the way a doctor might deliver a diagnosis. "An essential part of my work in your mother's home is ensuring that every element of this property meets the latest building code requirements as defined by our local governing bodies. This doorknob needs to be replaced, pronto."

My mind reeled. Was Mom behind this? Had she complained about the lock, asked Lance to deal with her difficult daughter? Or was this all Lance—another move in whatever game he was playing, determined to erase any boundary I tried to establish?

"I want to see this residential building code that supposedly governs doorknobs," I said, straightening my back. "Until you show it to me, I want you to leave my door alone."

His expression went blank—not angry, not defensive. Just . . . empty. Like a mask slipping off to reveal nothing underneath. The absence of emotion was somehow more chilling than anger would have been.

"Have it your way, Jessica," he said, his words as empty as his gaze.

We stared at each other. The silence stretched on. It was only a few seconds, but it felt like minutes, hours. But I refused to look away, to be cowed, even though I felt my knees trembling.

Mom's jovial voice from downstairs broke the tense silence.

"Oh, Lance!" she said. "How do you like your eggs, dear?"

Lance blinked and smiled at me, the charm mask back on.

"Time for breakfast," he said. "Mom is such a sweetheart, isn't she?"

He turned on his heel and strode away with heavy footsteps, his words circling in my head.

Now he was calling her Mom, too?

21: JESSICA

Confronting Mom about her financial arrangements with Lance while he was still in the house would be disastrous. She'd get defensive, side with him, and make me the bad guy for questioning her judgment.

So I retreated. For now.

But through my locked door, I heard them chatting away downstairs faintly. And I caught the tantalizing salty-sweet aroma of bacon drifting upward to my room. My stomach grumbled, but since I was fasting, I couldn't eat anything until the afternoon. I'd picked a terrible time to start a new diet.

Still, my head was spinning. He was installing smart locks? A security system? Mom had never expressed any interest whatsoever in adding any of that stuff to her house. There were a dozen other more pressing repairs Lance could have been working on, yet he started with a fully equipped security system with a bunch of cameras?

It made no sense. It felt like a brazen attempt to pad the bill with unnecessary services.

When he was gone, I had to find a diplomatic way to question her about this.

I settled at my desk again and started research into Melody Rockwell's immediate family.

According to Melody's obituary: "*She is survived by her parents, Robert and Margaret Rockwell, and her dear older sister, Ingrid . . .*"

But that had been written ten years ago. I found, sadly, two new obituaries since then.

Robert Rockwell's obituary appeared first. Five years ago. "*Survived by his beloved wife, Margaret, and daughter, Ingrid.*" The photo showed a balding man with kind eyes and a cautious smile.

Margaret Rockwell died only one year after her husband. "*She is survived by her devoted daughter, Ingrid, and was preceded in death by her husband, Robert, and daughter Melody.*"

Only Ingrid, Melody's older sister, was left. Hopefully.

I searched for Ingrid Rockwell, my fingers moving faster now.

Her Facebook profile loaded first. Ingrid Rockwell-Thomas, owner of Rio Nail Lounge on Main Street in downtown Newnan. The business page was active—hundreds of followers, recent posts featuring nail art designs, customer testimonials, pics of a cheerful staff.

Ingrid appeared in several photos: late forties or early fifties, with dark, shoulder-length hair and a smile that seemed genuine despite everything she'd lost. She looked . . . normal. Approachable.

I knew exactly where the salon was located; I had driven past it several times recently during my forays into the town's business district. The nail lounge had caught my eye, with its turquoise awning and the artistic nail designs painted across the front window. I'd even thought about stopping in for a manicure.

Now, I had a better reason to visit.

But would she talk to me about Lance?

According to the business hours, the salon opened at 9:30 AM on Saturdays. They had opened five minutes ago.

I called the number before I lost my nerve. A girl who sounded like a teenager answered.

"Rio Nail Lounge, this is Chloe. How can I help you?"

"Hi, is Ingrid available?" I asked. My voice sounded steadier than I felt.

"Do you have an appointment today?" Chloe said.

My mind went blank. "No, I—"

"Ms. Ingrid will be back on Monday, ma'am. We can fit you in now if you can swing by in the next fifteen minutes, or I can schedule you with one of our other technicians—"

"I'll make an appointment for Monday," I said, "with Ms. Ingrid, please. For a manicure—I'll take whatever slot she's got available."

"Sure thing. I'll book you for eleven if that works for you."

"Eleven is perfect."

With the appointment booked, I shifted to my legal pad beside my computer. Writing things down by hand always helped me think and had the strange effect of relaxing me sometimes, as if by going through the trouble of writing with pen and paper I was putting things in order.

I jotted down what I'd learned so far, which wasn't much. But it was a start.

All About Lance Cutler:

He found out Mom's house is paid off and she holds the release of lien. (Why would he care?)

Limited digital footprint. Seems deliberate.

All HandyHelper clients appear to be older women.

One client accused him of being too pushy and blocked his number. (Too bad I can't talk to her.)

Married for three years to Melody Rockwell and then she dies, not sure how. He said she had cancer, but is that true? He's not named in her obituary. Possibly a nasty divorce. Odd.

Rapping the end of my ballpoint pen against my bottom lip, I studied my list. There was nothing here that I could present to my mother yet. As Junior would have said: *A tad bit too circumstantial, Sis.*

But I felt like I was onto something. Possibly something bigger than just Mom. What if . . .

No . . . Focus on the facts, Jess.

Downstairs, I heard Lance getting to work.

It sounded like a drill boring into the walls.

22: JESSICA

On Sunday, I decided to attend church with my mother. We needed to spend time together outside of the house. The house and Lance had become a powder keg between us, and I wanted a safe, neutral place to interact with her.

Yesterday, after Lance had finished installing the "fully equipped security system" and finally left, I toured the house. I'd found a sleek control panel embedded in the wall near the front door, and Ring cameras posted in the veranda and out back above the deck, their shimmering digital eyes tracking every movement.

There was a high-tech smart lock on the front door, too, the numeric keypad backlit with a soft glow.

I'd found Mom in the kitchen, stirring something in a glass mixing bowl. It looked like she was making a cake. Since Lance had started coming around, she spent more time in the kitchen than ever before.

"So," I said. "Now you have a security system."

"It's wonderful, isn't it?" Mom said. "I feel safer already, Jessie. Everything can be controlled from my phone—Lance set it all up for me."

I'd need to figure out how to get the app on my phone, too—without his "help."

"Do you have the PIN for the control panel, Mom? So I can switch it on and off?"

"Lance wrote it down for you on a Post-it. It's on the counter there."

I turned to the island and saw a four-digit code written carefully on a note.

"Lance wrote this?" I asked. "The PIN is supposed to be private."

She smiled at me as if I were dense. "He already had a key, remember? Speaking of which, he installed a smart lock on the front door. The PIN for both the alarm and the panel are the same."

"How convenient," I said, but I bit my tongue against what I wanted to say.

At eight o'clock the next morning, Sunday, I was already dressed and sipping coffee in the breakfast nook when Mom came downstairs in a navy-blue dress, black flats, and full makeup. Her eyes widened at my appearance.

"You're coming to church with me?" she asked.

"We need some mother–daughter time outside the house. We can go to brunch afterward, too, at Caswell's Corner if you'd like."

She beamed brighter than she had in days. I felt as if the frost between us since Friday had thawed.

But the ten-minute drive to church tested me: As I drove, Mom talked incessantly about Lance. *He's such a nice young man, so knowledgeable. He's going to fix and upgrade everything for us, Jessie. I'm so happy that you hired him for that first job and we reconnected with him.*

I finally cranked up the volume on the radio, which happened to be playing gospel music, and she stopped blathering about the handyman and hummed along with the soft melody.

I hadn't been to First Baptist in ages, but the building was nicer and larger than I remembered: a gigantic sanctuary with glistening mahogany pews and majestic stained-glass windows. As we settled into our seats, Mom leaned over to me and said in a conspiratorial whisper: "Lance has completed major renovation projects for the church as well. Did you know that?"

"No." I gritted my teeth and scanned the gathering crowd. What if Lance was lurking here, too?

If he was, I didn't see him. After the service concluded, I gently steered Mom back to my car. She wanted to socialize, and after her first embarrassing "My daughter recently moved back home with me" remark to a friend, I couldn't stand lollygagging in the crowded foyer with her for the next twenty minutes while she told everyone about my failures.

At the brunch spot, Caswell's Corner, we settled into a corner booth. It was too early for mimosas so we both ordered tea. Many customers were dressed in their Sunday best, and soft piano jazz played on the audio system as the waitstaff bustled back and forth.

"This has been a fine morning," Mom said. "Such a treat. Thank you."

"It's how I envisioned moving back in with you would be," I said. "Spending quality time with you, one-on-one. We don't do that often enough."

"I've always been right here, Jessie." Mom made a here-I-am gesture with her hands.

"We should schedule regular outings like this."

"That sounds lovely." Mom raised the laminated menu, glanced over the edge of it at me. "You know, if I recall correctly, Lance's mother used to manage this restaurant."

I let out a soft hiss. "Can we please *not* talk about Lance? I was enjoying the moment."

"I don't understand your grudge against this man. It perplexes me."

"All right, then." I set down my ceramic teacup. "How much are you paying him for all this work he's been doing? Like installing smart locks and a new security system? You never said anything before about wanting those things."

"We need to ensure our safety. Two women living alone on the edge of town . . ."

It sounded exactly like what Lance had said to me, verbatim.

"But how much does it all cost, Mom?"

"That's none of your business."

"You're on a fixed income. You get the pension from teaching, Social Security, whatever Dad had left in his retirement fund . . . but you're not rolling in cash, and Lance isn't working for free."

"If you insist on knowing, I've committed a portion of the rent you're paying to funding these home improvements."

I blinked. "Then it's like I'm paying him to be there."

"You're paying rent—and a very reasonable rent at that," Mom said. "What I do with that money is none of your concern."

"Is that all you're paying him? Can I see your contract with him, just to be sure?"

Her eyes flared. "I'm not senile, Jessie. You seem to be implying that I don't know how to manage my own affairs."

"Mom, you can't trust Lance. I'll prove it to you."

"Prove it, then." Her voice cracked like a whip. "What actual, credible evidence against this man do you have?"

"I'm still working on that."

Mom's brittle, mocking laughter cut me like a blade. I lowered my gaze and stared into my teacup. Why had I brought this up?

At that tense moment, the server stopped by the table. He saw the looks on our faces and said in a hesitant tone, "If this is a bad time, I can come back in a few minutes, ladies."

"We're perfectly fine here." Mom put down the menu and put on an artificial smile that didn't reach her eyes. "My daughter and I have settled our petty disagreement, and we'll be ordering our meals now."

We barely spoke for the rest of the day.

23: JESSICA

On Monday, I hoped to get the "actual, credible evidence" about Mr. Lance Cutler that might finally convince my mother to take me seriously.

My nail appointment at Rio Nail Lounge on Main Street was at eleven o'clock, but I had an earlier appointment at another business in the same area: a newly opened coffee shop where the owner had agreed to hear my pitch for a social media marketing campaign. Despite the chaos at home—despite Lance's shadow stretching across every room of Mom's house—I was determined to make progress building my freelance career. My severance funds weren't going to last forever, and the thought of being financially dependent on anyone, especially in this situation, made my stomach clench.

The pitch went well. The owner signed a contract on the spot for a ninety-day campaign. Another win. Things were trending upward with JT Marketing Consulting. Would that same luck carry over to persuading Melody's older sister to talk to me about Lance?

I arrived about ten minutes early at the nail salon, my palms already damp. The interior was designed like a spa: soft peach and cream walls, comfortable leather chairs, glass tables with fresh orchids, and gentle instrumental music drifting from hidden speakers. A tall display case full of dozens of colorful bottles of nail polish occupied a prominent position in the waiting area.

The air smelled of acetone beneath a heavy layer of lavender and eucalyptus, the competing scents making my sinuses tingle. It was busier than I'd expected for a late Monday morning—all six stations occupied by nail technicians bent over their clients' hands, the low hum of conversation and the occasional burst of laughter creating an intimate atmosphere.

A tender-faced woman in her early twenties sat behind the front desk, her own nails painted a glossy coral. Her nametag read CHLOE. She smiled as she checked me in.

"Ms. Ingrid will be with you as soon as she finishes her current client, ma'am. Please have a seat."

I recognized Ingrid from her Facebook photo: She worked at a station in the far corner of the salon, partially screened by a decorative bamboo divider. She was chatting away with her current client, laughing and smiling, her hands moving with practiced efficiency. A positive sign—she was in a good mood.

Still, my knee bounced against the waiting room chair, that bad nervous habit I'd never broken, while I mentally rehearsed what I was going to say. *Will you talk to me about your dead sister's ex, please? I hired him as a handyman and now we can't get rid of him. Any tips?*

That sounded terrible. But so would anything else.

A few minutes later, Ingrid wrapped up her appointment and strolled over to me with a welcoming smile. She was petite, maybe five-three, with sparkling dark eyes and the kind of effortless beauty that probably made tipping generously an instinct for her clients.

"Hello there, Jessica. I'm Ingrid. First-time customer?"

"I am."

We shook hands—hers were impossibly soft, mine still clammy—and she guided me to her station. The chair was positioned near the window, afternoon sunlight filtering through sheer curtains and casting everything in a warm glow. On her workstation, a framed photo showed a younger Ingrid with another woman who looked like Melody—same delicate features, same smile.

It saddened me.

We made small talk as I settled into the chair. Ingrid adjusted her rolling stool and reached for my hands with gentle confidence.

"You've got a bit of damage here." She studied my fingers, focusing on the nail I had damaged while replacing the smoke alarm battery on move-in day at Mom's house. Her touch was professional but kind as she turned my hand. "Looks like you had a run-in with something sharp."

"I was trying to play handyman for my mom." I forced a chuckle, but sensed an opening. My heart rate kicked up a notch. "We ended up hiring a real handyman for a flooding issue, though. He did a good job—Lance Cutler. I hear he works quite a bit around town, too."

The change was instantaneous. Ingrid's fingers stiffened against my palm, just for a beat, before she continued her examination. Something shifted in her eyes, too—a wariness, maybe even fear.

"Does he?" Her voice remained pleasant, but I heard the control beneath it. "I'm not familiar with the name."

Now, she was outright lying to me. She was his ex–sister-in-law. Why not fess up? The air between us felt heavy, charged with unspoken things. The lavender scent seemed cloying now instead of soothing.

"Lance and I actually went to Newnan High together, but I didn't remember him," I said. "He was a year ahead of me."

I noticed a slight tightening of her jaw. She reached for a bottle of cuticle oil, her movements precise but no longer relaxed.

I said, "He was dating Melody—"

Ingrid's gaze snapped to mine, her pupils dilating. Her voice dropped to barely above a whisper, taut as a rope. "What are you here for? Did *he* send you?"

Did he send me? What was she talking about?

Shaking my head, I lowered my voice, too. "I only want information about Lance. I know he married your sister, may she rest in peace. But he wasn't listed in the obituary—"

"They were divorced. Mel's been gone for ten years." She studied me with eyes that had seen something she didn't want to revisit. "We didn't want his name in her obit. Anyway, you say he didn't send you, and maybe I believe you."

"Why would he send me to you? I don't understand."

"Forget I said that. Are you trying to date him, then?"

"Date him?" I almost laughed, the sound catching in my throat. "God, no. He did ask me out—"

"You should stay away from him." Her gaze darted toward the salon's entrance as if she worried Lance might materialize in the doorway. Sunlight glinted off the glass front, making me squint.

"Why?"

"Bad news. All around." She looked away, her gaze unfocused, seeing something I couldn't. Then she blinked, focused on me again. "What am I doing for you here today, Jessica? I can offer you some suggestions if you'd like."

"Please." I leaned forward in my chair. Around us, the salon continued its gentle rhythm—the soft brush of files against nails, the quiet conversation at other stations, the trickle of water from somewhere in the back. "My mom has hired him to work at her house, indefinitely. I don't trust him and want him out, but she won't listen to me. He's charmed her."

"Of course he has." A sad smile twisted Ingrid's lips, making her look years older. "He's very good at that."

"I need to convince her to get him out. If you can tell me something, or talk to her yourself—"

"I suggest a basic nail package for today," Ingrid said and put on a synthetic smile. "We need to work on your overall nail health right now, Jessica. Looks like it's been a while since you've had a professional manicure."

I leaned back in the chair. Why wouldn't she talk to me? Clearly, she knew something explosive about Lance. What was her reluctance all about?

"I'll leave you with my card." I pulled one of my business cards from my purse. I balanced it on top of her workstation. "If you change your mind about discussing this, please call me, text me, whatever. I could really use your help."

Ingrid glanced at the card, but made no attempt to pick it up. She swiveled back to me and flipped on a smile that didn't reach her eyes.

"Basic nail package it is, then," she said.

I sat there for the next forty minutes, making polite conversation while Ingrid worked on my nails with professional efficiency. She shaped, buffed, and polished, her hands steady and sure, but we both knew the real conversation was over. Whatever Ingrid knew about Lance Cutler—whatever had happened to Melody—would remain locked behind that careful smile and those frightened eyes.

When I left the salon, my nails looked better than they had in months. But my hands shook as I gripped the steering wheel, and Ingrid's words echoed in my mind:

Did he send you?

You should stay away from him.

I couldn't make sense of what she'd said.

I glanced in my rearview mirror as I pulled away from the curb. I could see Ingrid standing near the salon's front door, my business card now in her hand, staring down at it like it might cut her.

Maybe she would call me. Maybe she wouldn't.

But I'd seen the fear in her eyes, and that told me everything I needed to know about Lance Cutler.

He was as dangerous as I suspected he was.

24: JESSICA

Late that night, strange noises pulled me out of an uneasy sleep plagued by bad dreams.

I'd dreamed about Lance, and it wasn't a romantic dream—he had trapped me inside a big wooden crate with steel bars, a homemade prison, and he gleefully pronounced he had "built it myself. I can fix and build anything—did you know that, Jessica?" While I struggled in vain to escape, grabbing the bars and rattling them and screaming, Mom approached and stood alongside Lance, her hand on his shoulder. They both regarded me curiously—like I was a feral, caged animal at the zoo . . .

An electronic sound woke me. It sounded like a soft beep.

Was that the security system?

I sat up, damp sheets falling away from me. Darkness swallowed my bedroom, except for a thin, glowing slice of blue at the bottom of my closed door. Mom kept a night-light glimmering outside in the hall. In the darkness, the blue hue had an unearthly pallor.

I reached for my phone on the nightstand, squinted when the brightness hit my eyes like needles.

3:17 AM.

Yesterday, I had managed to install the security system app on my phone. I fumbled to open it.

According to the app, the alarm was disengaged. I didn't recall turning it on before I'd gone to bed. I had assumed Mom would take care of it since she claimed she wanted the security system in the first place.

But the exterior cameras for the front and back door had gone dark as well. The status for each read: *Offline.*

A glitch? Or something else?

My heart knocked. Grabbing my phone like a weapon, I slipped out of bed and padded across the room, my oversized Atlanta Falcons T-shirt drifting around my legs.

Before bed, I'd locked my door. I pressed my ear against it.

I heard footsteps moving downstairs: heavy and deliberate. I recognized that methodical gait, the weight of it, immediately.

It was Lance.

You should stay away from him.

I shivered.

What was he doing in our house at 3:17 in the morning? How could he possibly think this was acceptable? How could Mom?

I disengaged the lock and pulled the door open a few inches, enough to poke my head out and look, and to hear better.

Mom's bedroom was located at the end of the hallway. The door was shut. I knew her sleep habits—she kept a sleep machine beside her bed, the rhythmic sounds of crashing ocean waves sometimes easing her into slumber. On other nights, fearful of insomnia, she washed down an Ambien.

I didn't want to wake her. I could handle this myself. *Had to* handle this myself.

Get out of our house, Lance. Right now. Or I'm calling the police.

That was all I had to say, but I couldn't make my legs move.

From downstairs, I heard another familiar sound: the clinking of metal tools.

He can't possibly be here working. Now?

I heard the soft whir of a drill.

The situation was so bizarre that, for a second, I was convinced that I was dreaming—that I had slipped from one bad dream into another one without realizing it. Handymen didn't show up at three o'clock in the morning to work. It was totally irrational.

It had to be a dream.

But my heart hammered so loudly that I heard blood rushing through my body, an ocean roar in my ears. If this was a dream, it was the most vivid one I'd ever experienced in my forty-three years on this earth.

Not a dream, Jess.

A deliberate tapping noise followed the whir of the drill. A hammer? Each tap measured, patient, like he had all the time in the world.

This is insane.

Drawing in a deep, shaky breath, I pushed open the door and walked to the edge of the staircase, my knees feeling wobbly. It was dark downstairs—usually, Mom left a light on in the first-floor hall-way, too.

From my vantage point, I couldn't see anything but shadows within shadows. I switched on the flashlight app on my phone and panned around the light beam, the white circle wavering with my trembling hand.

No one lurked at the bottom of the staircase. I saw only the hard-wood floor, its polish reflecting my light like dark water, the usual furniture casting strange shadows.

"Who's there?" I asked, and my voice crackled on the words.

The tapping ceased.

But no one answered.

"Lance?" I said. "If you're not out of this house in sixty seconds, I'm calling the police."

The drill whirred again. Mocking me.

"I mean it," I said, my voice steadier. "I will report you for tres-passing. You *will* be arrested."

The drilling stopped. I heard the clatter of metal tools—deliberate, unhurried, like he was packing up after a normal day's work. Footsteps, moving faster now—approaching the staircase with purpose.

I steeled myself—and he was suddenly there at the bottom as if he'd materialized from the shadows themselves. Crisply dressed in a work shirt that looked freshly pressed and jeans with a razor-sharp crease down the front. Looking well-scrubbed and professional, like he'd just stepped out of a shower. The normalcy of his appearance at this ungodly hour made everything feel more wrong, like reality had tilted off its axis.

He gazed up at me and smiled—that practiced smile that never quite reached his eyes.

I sucked in a breath.

"You need to leave," I said.

"A handyman's work is never done. I believe I told you that. I woke up and remembered a minor adjustment I needed to make. Couldn't get back to sleep until I'd completed it. You understand that feeling, don't you, Jessica? When something's not quite right?"

The way he said it, like we were alike, like he knew my mind, made my skin crawl.

"I want you out of here."

He clicked his tongue. "Mom's house. Mom's rules. I've got unrestricted access to all areas of the property, at all times, for work purposes—you'd know that if mommy allowed you to review our contract."

My head pounded.

He's lying, I thought.

But I wasn't so sure. He sounded too confident, and as he pointedly reminded me, I hadn't laid eyes on this agreement of theirs. Who knew what Mom had agreed to these days? What fine print she'd overlooked?

"Your legs are quite toned and attractive, Jessica. Lovely. All that exercise is paying off." He flicked his tongue across his lower lip, grinned like we were sharing a secret.

I realized I was standing there with only a big T-shirt on, showing entirely too much bare skin to this creep. My face burned.

Whistling softly—some tune I didn't recognize, melancholy and wrong—he swiveled away. I heard him let himself out, the door closing with a gentle click.

I pounded down the steps, my feet slapping across the cold wood.

When I glanced out the front window, I saw his van grumbling away down the drive, the taillights glowing like eyes. I flipped on lights and searched downstairs. I had no idea what he'd supposedly been working on. But the air smelled different—like sawdust and that raw, musky odor of him, marking territory.

My heart still raced.

I couldn't do this anymore. I *had* to get this man out of here, out of our lives.

To do that, I would have to take a step that I dreaded.

I needed to call Mitch.

25: JESSICA

Early that Tuesday morning at the high school track, instead of walking as I usually did, I ran.

Your legs are quite toned and attractive, Jessica.

Lance's words from our last encounter coiled through my mind like smoke. I grimaced as I pushed myself through laps, my heart pounding hard enough to hurt, my thigh muscles burning with each stride, sweat streaming down my face and stinging my eyes. As if I could burn away the memory of Lance standing in the house at three in the morning through grueling physical effort.

The track stretched endlessly before me, each stretch blurring into the next. My breathing came in harsh gasps that scraped my throat raw. Other early morning exercisers—a few dedicated runners, an elderly couple walking hand in hand—gave me a wide berth as I pounded past them, probably wondering what demon was chasing me.

I managed to run for three and a half laps before I felt so light-headed I knew I needed to stop or else I would collapse in a heap right there on the track. I slowed to a plodding walk, my legs trembling. After my heart rate had slowed, I wandered over to the nearby bleachers and collapsed onto the metal seats with my water bottle and towel.

I mopped my face dry and took slow, measured sips.

The run had cleared my head—not of Lance's intrusion, but of any remaining hesitation about what I needed to do.

I didn't want to talk to Mitch—I'd promised myself I would never speak to him again. He had called and texted me at least five times since our divorce had been finalized, and I'd never answered.

But involving my ex, for the sake of my mother and my own sanity, was my best shot.

Mitch worked for one of the largest credit reporting agencies in the country: DataSmart Solutions. He was a senior fraud investigator, which meant he had access to databases I couldn't dream of. His company tracked everything about everyone: credit histories, employment records, address changes, even social media patterns. He'd once bragged that he could piece together someone's entire life story from the digital breadcrumbs they left behind.

He was the closest thing I had to a CIA contact.

I slid my phone out of the nylon pouch clipped to my waist. Instead of calling Mitch, I called Claire.

She answered on the first ring. I heard the smooth purr of her BMW's engine and muted pop music in the background—probably her guilty pleasure playlist she only played alone. She was doing her morning commute from Fayetteville to her law office.

"Hey, morning," she said, her voice carrying that alert cheerfulness of someone already on their second coffee. "You never call this early. Everything okay?"

"I'm about to do something I vowed I never would, and I want you to talk me out of it."

"Whoa. What's going on?" The music clicked off.

I hadn't talked to Claire in a week or so. I gave her the highlights: Lance's escalating visits, Mom's blind trust, the latest intrusion at three in the morning.

"I'm so sorry, Jess," she said. "I'd no idea you were dealing with all this stress over a freakin' handyman."

"It's been a nightmare." I blotted perspiration from my forehead. "I don't want to get Mitch involved, but I feel like I'm at that point."

"Would Mitch help you, though?" I could hear Claire shifting into attorney mode, her voice taking on that careful tone she used when discussing the law. "He's straitlaced about his job. He couldn't launch any sort of investigation without getting permission from whomever is involved—proper authorization, documented reason for the search, all that red tape."

Count on Claire, the veteran lawyer, to raise a logistical concern I should have thought of myself.

"I hadn't thought about that."

"If Mitch agrees to help you in the first place, which he probably won't knowing how things ended between you two, he could get in serious trouble," Claire said. "Accessing those databases for personal use? That's termination at minimum, possible criminal charges at worst. I know it sounds terrible, Jess, but you may want to sit tight until this Lance character either finishes these jobs or screws up so badly your mom comes around to your way of thinking."

I watched a Coweta County maintenance truck circle the high school parking lot, its headlights cutting through the early morning haze. "Wait and see seems too risky, Claire. I think this guy has bigger plans than just finishing the job and moving on to the next client."

"Do you think he's sophisticated enough to orchestrate some elaborate financial scam? I've never met him. What's your gut tell you?"

I paused, gnawing my bottom lip. My mind flashed back to Lance leering at me at three o'clock in the morning.

"That I need to get him out of the house," I said. "No matter what it takes."

"Mitch probably won't get involved, though," Claire said, her concern evident even through the phone. "And if he does, he won't do it out of the goodness of his heart—he'll want something from you. You know how he is. He'll use this as leverage, try to worm his way back into your life. You may want to think about that, girl. I think you should keep Mitch out of it."

"You're absolutely right," I said. "Good advice."

But I'd already made up my mind. Some prices were worth paying when the alternative was having Lance Cutler continue to invade my life, the house, my sense of safety. Even if that price meant opening a door to Mitch that I'd fought so hard to close.

I scrolled to my Contacts list. My new name for Mitch stared back at me: *Cheater.*

"I hope I don't regret this," I whispered to myself.

I clicked his number.

26: JESSICA

The following evening, around five thirty, I found myself at what used to be one of my favorite haunts: S&J's Seafood and Oyster Bar, a restaurant in Buckhead that I'd last visited with my ex-husband, Mitch. Mitch and I would often meet there after work for dinner and cocktails.

And there I was again, planning to meet him.

Claire had warned me: Asking Mitch for anything would come with strings attached. Thick, tangled strings that would wrap around my throat like a noose. When I'd called him about my handyman problem, Mitch refused to discuss details over the phone. He wanted to see me. In person. At our old spot.

I was so desperate, I agreed to it.

I'd dressed down deliberately: a plain black blouse that showed no curves, gray slacks with a conservative cut, black flats I'd worn to a funeral two years ago. I'd pulled my hair into a tight bun that tugged at my scalp, applied minimal makeup—just enough to avoid looking haggard—and skipped the jewelry. Nothing that glittered, nothing that invited his gaze to linger. I needed him to see me as a professional contact, not an ex-wife he could still manipulate.

The restaurant had an upscale vibe: soft light, luxurious seating, mahogany accents, and a gleaming glass case full of oysters that caught your eye the moment you stepped inside. The happy hour crowd was already there, lingering over oysters on the half-shell and pricey drinks.

Mitch was already there, too, seated at our usual table in the far corner. Some habits, apparently, died hard. He stood when he saw me approaching, and I registered the details against my will: his meticulously trimmed hair, how his crisp white golf shirt fit his long, slender physique, the fit of his tailored navy-blue slacks, his leather shoes polished to a mirror shine. He'd always been punctual and well-dressed. Those qualities hadn't changed.

He stood to meet me.

"Wow, you look fantastic, Jess," Mitch said.

The lie hung between us, obvious and graceless. I looked like someone who'd purposely made herself unattractive, and we both knew it.

We exchanged a brief hug, cordial and stiff, our bodies remembering the choreography even as our minds resisted. His cologne enveloped me—that woody fragrance I'd bought him for Christmas two years ago, the one that had always mingled perfectly with his natural scent. My body responded before my brain could stop it: a flutter low in my belly, a treacherous warmth spreading through my chest.

Probably his girlfriend loves the fragrance, too, I thought, and felt my gut winding up. I blew out a deep breath.

"Thanks." I settled across from him.

"You've been working out, hmm?" His gaze traveled over me with an appraising look I remembered too well.

"Life goes on. JT Consulting is keeping me quite busy. I have six clients now."

His eyebrows arched. "Impressive. I always knew you could make self-employment work."

I placed my leather organizer on the table and unzipped it. He glanced at it.

"Right down to business, eh, Jess?" He lifted his martini glass—gin, three olives, the way he always ordered it—and sipped, watching me over the rim. He signaled the server hovering nearby. "Don't you want a drink?"

"I've got an hour-long drive back to Newnan ahead of me later. Water is fine."

A slight nod. "I already put in an order for the appetizer we like. The oysters Rockefeller."

Of course he had. He was reminding me of our shared history, of the intimacy we'd once had, of all the meals we'd shared in this spot. I shrugged, but my stomach betrayed me with a low growl. I'd been fasting all day and had finally reached my eating window.

"Thanks for taking the time to meet with me," I said, as if we were there for a business meal and nothing more. "I need your professional advice."

"Shoot."

For the next ten minutes, I told him everything, starting with the plumbing disaster that had brought Lance into our lives in the first place. I detailed his growing encroachment, his influence over my mother, and my amateur investigation that so far had yielded nothing concrete.

Mitch listened without interrupting, his expression shifting from casual interest to genuine concern. He nodded at key points, murmured "Hmm" and "I see" at others.

The oysters arrived as I was wrapping up, steam rising from the shells filled with spinach, bacon, Parmesan, and cream sauce. The aroma made my mouth water.

"Well?" I asked. "Is this something you can help me with? Can you dig up some details on this guy?"

Mitch plucked an oyster from the platter and seasoned it with a squeeze of lemon and a dash of Tabasco sauce. "My work laptop is back at my place."

There it was. The hook I'd known was coming.

Of course he hadn't brought his computer. He needed a reason to reel me in deeper, to extend our time together beyond this public space. To get me into his apartment, where the boundaries would blur and the past might come rushing back to complicate the present.

"But will you help?" I asked.

"You'll need to come back to my apartment."

I picked up two oysters and placed them on the small appetizer plate. I forced myself to eat slowly, despite feeling ravenous enough to devour the entire platter.

"It's only because my work laptop is there," he added, his voice taking on that reasonable tone I knew so well. The tone that suggested I was being paranoid to question his motives.

"As long as you understand nothing's going to happen."

He scowled. "Give me a little credit, will you, Jess? I know you better than you think."

"What does that mean?"

"I know you're never going to forgive me."

I put down my fork. "Then why do you keep calling? Texting?"

"It's not complicated." He sipped his martini, grimaced as if it suddenly tasted bitter. "I just don't want you to hate me anymore."

There were a dozen possible responses to that remark. Like: *Then you shouldn't have cheated on me, Mitch.* And: *Don't bother—I'll always hate you.* And: *Why do you care if I hate you? We're divorced.*

But would any of those snappy comebacks change how I felt? Would any of it repair the irreparable damage between us?

The server materialized at our table, pad in hand, giving me an excuse not to answer.

"I'd like the New England clam chowder," I said. "And the shrimp-and-scallops salad, please, dressing on the side. I'm famished."

Mitch ordered the blackened red snapper, but barely took his gaze away from me, those dark eyes that had once looked at me with love now studying me like I was a puzzle he was determined to solve.

"Did you hear what I said?" he asked when the server left. "I don't want you to hate me anymore."

"Do you remember that old Rolling Stones song? How does it go? You can't always get what you want, Mitch."

He lowered his gaze, reaching for another oyster, but I saw the muscles in his jaw stiffen. I felt a small spark of triumph. It was a minor victory in a pointless conflict, but I'd take it.

The question was whether accepting his help tonight would cost me more than I could afford to pay.

27: JESSICA

I had never seen Mitch's new apartment, and hadn't expected to, either. But then again, I'd never expected to be divorced and living back home with my mom.

Life kept throwing curveballs at me.

It was a one-bedroom in Dunwoody, less than a mile away from the townhome community where we'd lived as a married couple. I recognized some of the same pieces of furniture that used to occupy our home—items Mitch had either brought in, or we had purchased together and agreed he could keep. The cognac leather couch where we'd binged so many TV shows (and had more than a few intimate encounters). The oak bookshelf I'd assembled one Sunday afternoon, cursing at the inscrutable instructions. And it felt strange seeing the coffee table I had ordered during a Wayfair sale sitting in this unfamiliar place, scratches and water rings still visible on its walnut surface.

The big windows overlooked a parking lot; a wooded area bordered the complex property. It was seven in the evening, and the sun would be setting soon. After we concluded our business, I had a long drive back home ahead of me.

I also didn't notice any signs of a girlfriend—no article of clothing like a hat, a scarf, or a pair of shoes. No wine glasses with a lipstick smudge on the rim. No feminine fragrance lingering in the air. Even as I did the quick scan, I questioned why I cared. We were divorced. He could date anyone he wanted.

"Nice apartment," I said. My voice sounded hollow in the space.

He shrugged, hands sliding into his pockets. "Thanks. I'd probably move back in with my folks, too, if they didn't live across the country. The rent here is astronomical."

"The downstream effect of bad decisions, hmph?" I couldn't resist. The words came out sharper than I'd intended.

He let my comment pass with a grunt, turned toward the breakfast nook. It was furnished with a glass-topped dinette table flanked by four mismatched chairs. I didn't recognize the pieces, so I assumed he had acquired them from a thrift shop.

He had set up his work laptop on the table, the screen already glowing. He offered me a glass of wine—which I politely declined—and I sat next to him as he rolled up his sleeves and logged into his company's network. His fingers moved quickly across the keyboard.

"We'll start by checking public records on your Mr. Cutler," Mitch said.

"I already did that."

"Maybe you missed something." His tone was patient, borderline condescending.

"I didn't. But whatever."

His long, slender fingers danced across the keys. I repositioned my chair so I could peer over his shoulder.

A tiny, loose thread lingered at the edge of his collar. I resisted the urge to pluck it off.

After a few minutes, Mitch stopped typing.

"You were right—there's not much." He stroked his clean-shaven chin. "I suspect our Mr. Cutler employs a data removal service."

"To keep himself off the web?"

Mitch nodded, sipped wine. "Data removal brokers will submit opt-out requests to people finder sites. They focus on data such as name, address, phone number, email. For people who want to remain hard to find."

"Which is strange for a small business operator, don't you think? What's he got to hide?"

"It won't be enough to convince Marilyn," Mitch said.

"A tab bit circumstantial," I said sourly, repeating Junior's snide remark. "Can you dig into private records?"

"Can I pull his credit?" Mitch turned, a frown creasing his face. "That's breaking the law. Fair Credit Reporting Act—I'd need to get Cutler's authorization to probe deeper."

"You don't mind breaking rules. You cheated on me."

He blushed. "I could lose my job over something like this, face criminal charges."

"Seriously?" I leaned back in the chair, crossing my arms over my chest. "So that's it, then? We're done? You asked me to come over so you can do a basic public records search that I already did myself?"

I started to rise from my seat.

"Hang on," Mitch said. "We're not done yet."

"What else is there?" I sank back into the chair.

"There's you." His eyes gleamed.

"What about me? Why are you looking at me like that?"

He smiled. "I do this work for a living. And I've got a hunch."

"About?"

"Send me a text," Mitch said. "In the text, write that you give me permission to pull your credit."

"Why—"

"Just roll with me on this, babe. Let me do my thing."

Babe. The word hung in the air between us, familiar and painful. Sighing, I took out my phone and pulled up my last text with Mitch. He glanced at the screen before I could angle it away.

"*Cheater?*" he asked. "That's your name for me in your phone, Jess?"

I stammered. "You weren't supposed to see that."

"I guess I deserve it." His shoulders drooped.

I sent him a text granting permission to do a credit check. He confirmed that he'd received the message on his phone and swiveled back to his computer. I peered over his shoulder as he typed in a flurry, my pulse quickening.

"Here we are," he said, like a magician pulling a dove from a hat. He pointed to a line on the screen with a timestamp in October. "On this day, Legacy Holdings, LLC, ran a soft inquiry on your credit. Does that sound familiar?"

My breath caught. I checked my phone, scrolled through a long list of messages. "That was the day I first contacted Lance! When the toilet flooded."

"And you're not familiar with Legacy Holdings?"

"I've never heard of them. Ever." My heart pounded. "The soft inquiry—anyone can do that on you, right?"

"Technically, yes." Mitch sipped his wine, his eyes shining brighter; he'd always been passionate about his work. "All that's needed for a soft pull are some identifiers like your name, date of birth, address—no Social Security Number required. Data brokers sell that sort of basic info or anyone could grab it online with a little research on most people. A soft check gives the requester a snapshot of your credit. Credit card companies use them all the time when they send folks those pre-approval letters in the mail. It doesn't impact your credit score like a hard pull, when you apply for a mortgage or a car loan, for example."

"Do you think it's Lance's company?"

"Looking." His fingers whirred on the laptop. "Well. Now this is something."

I had risen to my feet so I could get a better look at the screen.

"The company is registered in Wyoming?" I asked.

"People use states like Wyoming to set up shell companies—laws there allow individuals to register an LLC privately. Whoever is behind Legacy Holdings set it up ten years ago."

"Is there any way you can see who owns it?"

Mitch shook his head. "Not even I can pierce that veil."

"But this shell company checked on me. The same day I called Lance for the first time." My mind raced. "That's not a coincidence."

He was nodding, fingers already moving across the keyboard again. "Whoever this guy is, he's a pro—or he's working with a pro. He's not the simple, helpful handyman he claims to be, Jess. Guys like that don't set up shell companies."

A pulse throbbed painfully in my temple. "I can't prove that he's behind it. Even if I could, what does it matter? Can we find anything useful on this company that proves it's scammy?"

Within only a few minutes, Mitch delivered more.

"Look at this," Mitch said. "This is one of our databases that pulls from public records of real estate transactions. Legacy Holdings has been collecting houses like freakin' Monopoly pieces. Check it out." He shifted the computer toward me.

I stared at the display. A list of residential addresses filled the screen, located in several different metro Atlanta cities, almost thirty properties total. The addresses were organized by date of acquisition, each one a data point in a growing empire.

Five of them were in Newnan.

My heart thundered.

"This *has* to be him," I said. "A mysterious company runs a soft check on my credit the same day I contact Lance, and this company happens to own a long list of houses, some of them literally next door to my mom?"

"Then, the company sells the houses," Mitch said, studying the display. "Checking here, it looks like within a year of acquiring a house, the property goes on the market—and fetches a *very* handsome price."

"Bilking them out of homes and then flipping them for healthy profits," I said. "What a perfect scam."

"How do you think he's picking up these properties?" Mitch asked, his voice distant.

"I don't know," I said. My hands had curled into fists, nails biting into my palms. Through the window behind Mitch, the last light drained from the sky, leaving only the harsh glow of parking lot lamps. "But I'll promise you: I'm not letting Mom's house be next on that list."

28: JESSICA

As I anticipated, Mitch asked if I wanted to spend the night at his place.

"It's dark, babe," he said, gesturing toward the window. Beyond the glass, the day had dissolved into a panorama of amber streetlights and velvet shadows. "You've got over an hour's drive ahead of you and you've had a long day."

"Mitch, I don't—"

"I'll sleep on the couch out here." He raised both hands in a do-no-harm gesture. "I won't touch you."

What surprised me was that I almost said "yes."

The word sat on the tip of my tongue. Not because I had any interest whatsoever in a one-night hookup with my ex-husband. And not because of the long drive stretching ahead of me, the endless ribbon of dark highway I'd have to navigate while exhaustion tugged at my eyelids.

It was Mom's house.

Her house had become a pressure cooker, the walls seeming to press inward every time I walked through the door. The air there felt thick, contaminated somehow, as if Lance's presence had seeped into the drywall. Being at Mitch's place—being anywhere else, really—felt like gulping fresh oxygen after holding my breath underwater.

But I'd checked the Ring camera on the app several times since I'd been gone. Lance had been there at the house for *hours*, his van parked in the driveway. I had no idea what he was doing there, but whatever it was, it wasn't good. Schemers like Lance didn't spend entire evenings at a "client's" home unless they were burrowing deeper, tightening their grip.

I had to go back. Mom needed me. Even if she didn't realize it yet.

"Thanks for the offer, but I've got to get home." I reached for my purse on the kitchen counter.

At the door, we exchanged a hug. His body felt familiar in a way that made my heart skip, and for a moment, I wished I hadn't reached out to him in the first place.

"Please keep me posted on how things go with Marilyn," he said, his breath warm against my hair. "I'm here for you, Jess. We'll work all of this out."

With Mitch's help, I had devised a new plan for approaching the Lance situation with Mom. It was a good plan—logical, measured, designed to avoid triggering her defensiveness. Whether it would actually work was another question entirely.

"We'll definitely be in touch," I said. "Thanks for everything."

He started to lean in for a kiss, and when I stepped back, recognition flashed across his face. He seemed to remember himself, remember us, remember that we weren't those people anymore.

"Drive safe," he said, something wounded flickering in his eyes. "Text me when you get in."

When I arrived back in Newnan, it was past nine o'clock. Lance's van was finally gone. I found Mom in the living room. The TV was on—some baking competition reality show on Netflix— and she had fallen asleep in her favorite chair, her head tilted back at an angle that would leave her neck stiff in the morning, her lips parted, a soft whistling sound escaping with each exhale. The remote control lay on the floor where it had slipped from her fingers.

In that vulnerable pose, Mom looked so frail my heart kicked.

I thought about that list of residential properties that Legacy Holdings had accumulated. I was convinced Lance was behind it and equally convinced he had swindled those homes from women exactly like my mother—aging, lonely, too trusting.

What had happened to those women, those unwitting victims?

Most folks, especially my parents' generation, the Boomers, had spent a lifetime in their homes, raised children and possibly grand-children in them. For a lot of them, it was their only source of finan-cial security in their golden years. The pinnacle of the American Dream.

And Lance was stealing it from them. Why? Pure greed? Some sick criminal pathology? What kind of person did that?

I picked up a throw pillow from the nearby sofa and eased it underneath her head, to give her some neck support. Her breath caught briefly in her throat, but she didn't awaken.

"I love you, Mama," I whispered, and kissed her forehead. Her skin felt like parchment paper beneath my lips.

She kept on sleeping, oblivious to my presence, lost in whatever dream had claimed her.

I pulled the plush blanket from the back of the couch and draped it over her shoulders, tucking it around her sides. Then I straightened and looked around the room—at the framed photos on the mantel and the walls, the decorative pillows, the hardcover novels she kept in the bookcase (she had read every title, of course), all the clutter that made this place uniquely our home—and wondered how much of it would still be hers a year from now.

If Lance had his way, probably none of it.

I won't let that happen, I vowed. *No matter what.*

29: JESSICA

L*ance was in here.*

Upstairs, my bedroom door was locked, as I'd left it.

But when I opened the door, flicked on the lights, and stepped inside, I felt the hairs stiffen at the nape of my neck.

At first glance, I didn't see anything out of place. The white duvet on my bed lay smooth and undisturbed, the decorative pillows arranged in their usual pattern against the headboard. My jewelry box sat on the dresser, lid closed. The closet door was shut. The windows were closed, the blinds drawn to precisely the same level I always left them—an inch from the sill.

I was the only one who had a key to this room. Both the original and the spare had been in my purse the entire time I was gone, zipped into the interior pocket. I hadn't left a backup hidden anywhere in the house—not under the doormat, not in a fake rock, not taped to the underside of the porch railing. Nowhere.

But as I scanned the room, I couldn't shake that sense of wrongness.

Was it all in my imagination? Had I tumbled from a state of reasonable suspicion to full-scale paranoia? Lance could not have gotten inside through a locked door, and there was no other way to get inside the room. I kept the windows secured, too.

But Lance had been in the house for several hours. It wasn't clear what he'd been doing, and I wasn't going to wake up Mom to ask. For what I had planned, I needed to maintain the meager shreds of credibility I still had with her when it came to the topic of her favorite handyman.

But what if he'd found a way to get inside?

I stepped toward my desk. Admittedly, I had a touch of OCD about the placement of items in my personal space. The Dell laptop always sat squarely in the center of the black desk pad, perfectly aligned with the pad's edges. The wireless mouse pad belonged to the right of the computer, positioned at exactly the same distance from the laptop's corner every single time—close enough to reach without stretching, far enough to avoid accidental contact. My yellow legal pad lived on the left side of the laptop, parallel, an inch away.

I leaned closer, my heart throbbing.

The laptop had been moved.

Just a quarter of an inch. Maybe less. But shifted to the left, no longer centered on the pad. The mouse pad, too—displaced by what couldn't have been more than a few centimeters, but enough.

The legal pad had been slightly disturbed, too—by a few centimeters. The pages were full of my scribbled notes documenting my investigation into Lance.

What if he'd read all my notes? Tried to use my computer?

From studying my handwritten notes alone, Lance would know exactly how much dirt I was unearthing about him.

My throat tightened.

But was I sure? Confident enough to wake up Mom and declare that items in my room had shifted less than an inch and Lance must be the culprit?

I gnawed my bottom lip until I tasted blood.

You're losing your grip, Jess. That's what's happening.

I eased into the desk chair and pressed my fingers to my temples.

Mom wouldn't believe me—I knew that. She'd practically mocked my accusation about Lance moving my underwear. This new charge would sound even more ludicrous.

I swiveled in the chair, slowly surveying the room, until I started to feel dizzy.

It had been a long day, full of driving and activity. I needed to rest, wake up in the morning with a clear head, and prepare my new strategy with Mom to get her on my side.

As for the possibility that Lance had somehow gotten inside my room, I had another plan in mind.

A plan that would give me proof.

Real, undeniable, *camera-recorded* proof.

The kind even my mother couldn't dismiss.

30: JESSICA

To execute my new plan with Mom, I needed to get her alone so we could talk. That simple task seemed more challenging than ever now.

Lance visited every day, three days in a row: Thursday, Friday, Saturday. He arrived early—by the time I returned from my early-morning workout at the high school track, his van was parked in the driveway. He stayed at the house *all day*, not leaving until nine o'clock, when Mom was already yawning and nodding off in her favorite chair, in no state for a serious discussion.

I did my best to avoid Lance. He smiled when we saw each other in passing around the house, flashing that artificial grin, but I noticed a fresh awareness in his gaze—a predatory watchfulness. I was convinced he knew I was plotting something and was determined to prevent it with his hostile occupation in our home. The air felt charged whenever we were in the same space, like the pressure drop before a storm.

I got up early on Sunday, with the intent to attend church with Mom again. Showered and dressed and ready to go by eight, sipping coffee downstairs, but by eight thirty, I still didn't hear Mom upstairs making the usual getting ready sounds: the creak of the floorboards, the soft hiss of the shower.

Frowning, I went upstairs. Her door was closed. I knocked twice, and opened it.

The bedroom was shadowed, the blinds closed against the morning sunshine. Mom was still in bed, bundled within sheets.

This was unlike her. She was typically an early riser, especially on Sundays.

An awful memory surfaced in my mind: Twelve years old and spending the week in Savannah with Nana, just the two of us together, and noticing she hadn't gotten up one morning at her usual time. Walking into her bedroom, not getting an answer. Touching her shoulder and feeling cooling skin . . .

I felt dizzy.

"Mom?" I said, my voice fragile as glass.

Nothing. No movement. The air in the room felt thick.

"Mom?" I asked again, but in a louder tone.

Mom stirred, the sheets rustling. I let out a sigh.

"Oh . . . overslept," Mom said, in a raspy whisper.

I knotted my hands in front of me. "I was going to take you to church."

"Yes . . . of course." She slowly peeled back the sheets with trembling hands. "I'll get ready, Mama. I'm sorry."

The word stopped me cold.

Mama?

My throat tightened, constricting like a fist. "It's Jessie."

"I know who you are." She struggled upright, her characteristic sass surging back like a protective barrier. Her eyes flashed with indignation. "I'm not senile, child."

But her hands shook as she reached for the edge of the mattress, and I saw fear flicker across her face before she masked it.

"Right." I exhaled, trying to release the tightness in my chest. "I'll be waiting downstairs."

31: JESSICA

After church, when we were walking back to my car, I offered to take Mom to brunch. My pulse quickened at the thought—there, finally, in the neutral territory of a restaurant, I could navigate the conversation I'd been rehearsing in my head for the past three days.

"I appreciate the invitation, Jessie, but Lance is coming over soon," she said. Her eyes sparkled with undisguised excitement. "He's going to show me paint samples that I need to decide on. He's going to repaint the *entire* house. I'm so thrilled."

I could have kicked myself. Of course he was coming over. He was there every day without fail. Did he have any other clients? A life of his own?

We got in the car. The interior was stifling; it was unusually warm for October. I started the engine and cranked up the A/C, but remained parked.

If I couldn't get Mom alone in a restaurant—away from Lance's influence, his ever-present shadow—I had to broach the topic right here. Right now.

I drummed the steering wheel. "Mom, I wanted to ask you something."

"We've been having a pleasant morning so far." Her voice turned sharp, a knife's edge I recognized from too many of our interactions lately. "Don't spoil it."

"It's not about what you think." *Not directly, anyway.*

"Oh?" Mom's furrowed brow smoothed. She shifted toward me in her seat, suddenly interested. "Now I'm intrigued."

"Every now and then, I run a credit report on myself. Sort of as a financial checkup, to make sure there's no identity theft or anything like that going on. I ran one the other day and a company I'd never heard of before had recently run a soft credit inquiry on me. Legacy Holdings."

Her eyes were fuzzy. "I've never heard of them."

"I hadn't, either. I was suspicious. When I told Mitch about it, he got concerned, too."

"You talked to your husband?" Her gaze brightened, snapping back to me with sudden intensity. Hope flickered across her features —pathetic, desperate hope that made my chest ache.

"*Ex*-husband," I said, the word bitter on my tongue. "But that's his field. He's looking into it for me." I paused, giving weight to the next part. "He also wanted me to ask you: When was the last time you'd reviewed your credit report, Mom?"

Mom's gaze went distant, as if she were looking through the windshield at something I couldn't see. "I hadn't been concerned. Does Mitch think I should do this?"

"That's his recommendation," I said carefully. "As a general checkup."

Please, take the bait.

"We haven't run our credit since your father was alive," Mom said. "He handled all the finances for us."

My heart squeezed. For a moment, I saw her not as my frustrating, stubborn mother, but as a widow, lost in a world that had moved on without her husband's hand guiding the wheel.

I took my phone out of my purse. "There are credit reporting apps these days. We can take a look right now."

"How much time will it take?" She checked her phone again. "Lance is coming soon."

"I'm opening an account for you this second."

I tapped and scrolled through the credit monitoring app. When the report request reached the point at which Mom needed to verify her identity by answering three questions about her financial history, she struggled to answer one about a department store credit card. She squinted at the phone's screen, her reading glasses still in her purse.

"Goodness, how am I supposed to remember that?" she asked with an impatient sigh. "I don't recall every credit card I've had over the past twenty years."

I glanced at the list of possible answers on the display. "You used to shop at Macy's all the time. Maybe that one?"

"Possibly I acquired for a card there. You know how the clerks would aggressively promote those offers."

"Let's go with it."

It must have been the right answer: *Identity confirmed* flashed on the display.

"That was correct," I said. "The report's on the way."

"Lance is on his way to the house as well." She wagged her phone at me. "He texted me."

My heart knocked. I was banking everything on this plan. If it failed, if there was nothing there, I was lost. Worse than lost—I'd be the paranoid daughter who couldn't let her mother be happy.

The report materialized on the screen. I scrolled to "Recent Inquiries." The list populated slowly, line by line.

And there it was.

"Well?" Mom said.

I resisted the impulse to smile as I handed the phone to her. "Legacy Holdings ran a soft inquiry on you, too."

"What does this mean?" As she stared at the screen, her face twisted in a mixture of confusion and worry. "Who are these people?"

It's your favorite handyman. The words were right there, pushing against my teeth. I had to literally bite my tongue to keep them in. But I couldn't overplay my hand. I'd made that mistake before with Mom, pushed too hard, showed my cards too early, and watched her defensive walls slam down.

"Let me take this back to Mitch." It was the answer I knew she wanted to hear. I shifted into Drive. "He'll know what to do."

32: JESSICA

When we arrived home from church, Lance's van was already parked in our driveway, like a chess piece claiming territory.

"Ah, he's already here." Mom's voice carried that pleased lilt that made my jaw tighten. "I so appreciate a punctual man."

I rolled my eyes. Lately, Lance backed his work van into my usual spot next to Mom's Toyota, as if he were a member of the family. It had been forcing me to position my car behind hers, and at the edge of the pavement, my right tires sinking into the grass.

"Why don't you get out here, before I park?" I said to Mom. "Or you'll have to walk in the mud with your church shoes on."

Mom opened the door. I touched her shoulder before she climbed out.

"By the way, what we discussed about your credit? Let's keep that between you, me, and Mitch, please."

"Hmph." Mom's eyes narrowed with suspicion, but she nodded. I didn't know how much she'd already shared with Lance about her finances, but I couldn't risk her telling him what we'd discovered.

I wanted the pleasure of doing that myself.

Through the windshield, I watched her make her way toward the house—careful steps in her good shoes, avoiding the muddy patches where rainwater still pooled.

Lance appeared at the front door before she'd made it halfway up the walk. He opened it wide, standing aside like a doorman at a hotel, ushering her into her own home with a sweeping gesture. He waved at me with theatrical cheerfulness.

I squeezed the steering wheel, resisting the impulse to flip him off.

After he shut the door, I parked in my new, second-tier spot: behind Mom's sedan but alongside Lance's van, my vehicle next to the driver's-side door of his. I should have been grateful the driveway was as spacious as it was. I could have been forced to park on the street.

I needed to get in touch with Mitch and share our discovery about Legacy Holdings, but first, I had another, final amateur sleuthing task on my agenda.

I got out of my car. Thanks to how I'd positioned my vehicle, from the front windows of the house, no one—including Lance—would see what I was about to do next.

My fingers trembled as I opened the camera app. Adrenaline, I told myself. Just adrenaline. I took a breath—pulled the air deep into my lungs, held it for a count of four, released it slowly.

I edged toward Lance's van.

Every manufactured vehicle included a VIN—vehicle identification number. It was imprinted on the dashboard, for easy access and visibility for anyone who needed to scan it.

VIN registration data was public information. Whether a personal owner or a commercial entity had registered the vehicle, that information would be revealed to anyone willing to pay a fee to search vehicle ownership records.

I was banking on a commercial entity being tied to his van's registration—another exhibit in the case I was trying to build. Grabbing a photo of the VIN on his van ought to take less than ten seconds.

Still, my heart rate kicked up a notch as I leaned over the side of the van, studying the windshield. If Lance came outside and caught me, how would I explain what I was doing?

Hurry up, then, Jess.

I found the number in the bottom right corner of the windshield. Zoomed in with my phone's camera and snapped three quick photos.

"Got you," I whispered to myself.

I turned away from the van.

Lance stood at the back of his vehicle. Watching me. The faint smile that didn't reach his eyes played on his lips.

"Are you looking for something?" he asked.

"There's a big blob of bird shit on your windshield."

His eyes gleamed. "That sort of discovery interests you, hmm?"

"I'm interested in all sorts of things, just like you are." I nodded toward the house. "Did you enjoy snooping around while we were away?"

"I'm an honest, hardworking handyman, doing everything I can to improve this home for you and your mother." He spread his hands, as if to show he was guileless. "One day, you'll appreciate it, Jessica."

I gave him a wide berth as I went inside the house. I hurried upstairs to my bedroom, unlocked the door, and marched to the bookcase.

Two days ago, I had hidden a tiny, Wi-Fi-enabled nanny cam amid the books and framed photographs arranged on the shelves. The video recording device was so discreet that if you didn't know it was there, you would struggle to notice it.

When I'd last checked, the cam had yet to capture any incriminating behavior. But Lance had been inside the house for about twenty minutes by the time Mom and I arrived from church—the Ring camera at the front door proved it. Had he taken advantage of the opportunity to somehow bypass my lock again, and snoop around?

Before I checked, I fired off a text message to Mitch with a photo attached.

Here's a pic of the VIN. Please do your thing so we can get this guy out of here.

33: JESSICA

By the next day, Monday, I had gathered everything I needed. Now, it all came down to timing.

I needed Lance and Mom in the same room together. Considering that he'd been visiting every single day for nearly a week, with no end in sight, the opportunity should arrive very soon.

I expected Lance to show up early that morning for the next round of work: house painting. But when I woke at six for my workout, I heard a steady rain pattering against my bedroom window.

This might delay things. Can't paint a house in the rain.

As an alternative to visiting the high school track, I used the elliptical machine Mom had bought with good intentions and kept unused in the garage. The machine was practically brand new.

I put the elliptical through its paces, pushing myself hard for forty-five minutes. When I came back inside, sipping water and wiping my face with a towel, I found Mom in the kitchen pouring a cup of coffee.

"Good morning," I said. In what I hoped was a casual tone, I added: "Is Lance coming today?"

"He texted me last night that, depending on the forecast, he may be delayed."

"Oh, that's a shame."

Her lips puckered as if she'd tasted a lemon. "Sarcasm doesn't suit you well, Jessie."

Later that morning, I had a business meeting scheduled with a pizzeria on Main Street. The spot was directly across from Rio Nail Lounge.

Ingrid hadn't contacted me since our awkward appointment a week ago. After my sales presentation at the pizza restaurant—another easy win for JT Consulting—I crossed the street, holding an umbrella against the persistent rainfall.

I'd pop in and say hello. I didn't necessarily need Ingrid's help, but I wanted to gently inquire if maybe she'd changed her mind—and when I shared with her what I'd discovered, it might motivate her to join my side.

When I stepped inside the salon, collapsing my dripping umbrella, I saw the same young girl, Chloe, at the reception desk. But I didn't see Ingrid at her station in the far corner.

"Hey there," I said. "I don't have an appointment today, but I was wondering if Ingrid is available? I saw her last week."

The girl's mouth tightened in a grim expression. "Unfortunately, Ms. Ingrid won't be in for a while. She had a pretty awful accident."

A chill gripped me.

"An accident?"

Chloe nodded. "Like, the brakes on her car went out or something. Some weird malfunction thing. She's been in the hospital." She sighed heavily, her eyes glassy with sudden tears. "We're all praying for her to pull through."

Some weird malfunction thing.

"That's . . . terrible," I said. I felt out of breath.

She blotted her eyes with a tissue. "I can book you with someone else."

"That's okay."

I left and got in my car. I stared out the rain-blurred window, trembling from an icy coldness that had sunk deep in my bones.

A week ago, I had pressed Ingrid about Lance. Made notes on my legal pad that included her name. Those same notes had been sitting on my desk the evening that I was convinced that Lance had somehow bypassed my door lock and rummaged through my things.

Now Ingrid was in the hospital fighting to live.

. . . the brakes on her car went out or something. Some weird malfunction thing . . .

Malfunction—or sabotage?

Several minutes passed before I stopped trembling enough to start the car.

34: JESSICA

The skies didn't clear until Wednesday. Lance arrived shortly after sunrise, before I left for the track: When I looked outside the front window, I saw him unloading paintbrushes and other equipment from his van, along with several cans of paint. He wore denim overalls and a baseball cap, as if he were a member of a painting crew.

He'd also blocked my car in the driveway, the rear bumper of his van only a foot or so from mine.

This was a first. Usually, he parked behind Mom's sedan, or if I was gone when he arrived, he parked in my spot next to her car—which was annoying on its own. Until now, he'd never deliberately barricaded my vehicle.

I debated stomping outside to confront him. But I realized: That was what he wanted. And I was done playing his game.

Today, we were going to take him down.

Mitch texted me around ten o'clock: *On the road now. Traffic stinks—it's gonna take over an hour.*

See you soon, I responded. *Park on the street, btw.*

Mitch had taken the day off work to join me at Mom's. It had been his idea. My first instinct had been to decline the offer, but then I flashed back to my discovery about Ingrid's mysterious "accident" and realized it might be a wise idea to have backup.

I didn't know how Lance would respond to being exposed.

In my bedroom, I opened the manila folder containing the documents I had gathered, the fruits of my investigation. Much of what I'd found was still circumstantial, but I had a smoking gun that I hoped would finally win Mom over to my side.

Through my bedroom window, I saw Mom trundling about in her garden, working her kale and arugula plants. Blissfully unaware of what was coming. I heard Lance on the northern side of the house, painting.

I'm an honest, hardworking handyman, doing everything I can to improve this home for you and your mother . . .

Mitch texted: *Pulling up now.*

I responded: *I'll be out in a second.*

35: MITCH

I hadn't ever expected to visit my mother-in-law's—*ex*–mother-in-law's—home again. The thought of stepping foot on Marilyn's property had seemed like something relegated to the distant past, filed away with other chapters of my life I'd assumed were closed for good. But here I was, cruising down familiar suburban streets, my stomach tight with an emotion I couldn't quite name. Anticipation? Dread? Maybe both.

Jessica needed me there for this. That's what mattered.

I was grateful for the opportunity to support her. Despite everything that had happened between us—the erosion of our marriage for which I took much of the blame, the paperwork signed just a few weeks ago, the lawyers who'd divided our shared life into neat columns—I still cared about her. Loved her, even, in the complicated way that didn't fit into the boxes our divorce decree had created. When she'd reached out to me about this "handyman situation," I hadn't hesitated to get involved.

I parked my Audi in front of Marilyn's house around eleven fifteen that morning. The neighborhood looked the same as it had the last time I'd been here, maybe six months ago. Established oaks lined the street, their branches shedding leaves as autumn took hold. The air smelled of fresh-cut grass.

I texted Jessie that I'd arrived.

As I got out of my car, I assessed the home that had been the target of this questionable "handyman," Mr. Lance Cutler.

The place looked better than it had in years. Dramatically better, actually. The hedges that had once grown wild and scraggly now stood trimmed into precise geometric shapes. The gutters gleamed, swept clean of the pine needles and debris that used to overflow after every storm. Fresh shingles dotted the roof where I remembered seeing bare patches. A soft, creamy coat of paint—the color reminded me of vanilla buttercream frosting—gleamed on the front of the house, replacing the dingy colors that had been peeling for as long as I'd known Marilyn.

My chest tightened. This guy was good. That's what made him dangerous.

Hands in my pockets, I walked down the long driveway, and took a closer look at Cutler's service vehicle. The Mercedes-Benz cargo van gleamed, not a speck of dust or a single dent marring its surface. I squinted, looking for markings. Nothing. No company name, no phone number, no decal identifying the purpose of the man's enterprise.

The blank canvas of that pristine black vehicle sent a chill down my spine despite the warmth of the day. Legitimate contractors advertised. They wanted business. This felt like deliberate anonymity.

"May I help you?"

I turned. Lance Cutler—it had to be him since Jessie said he always worked alone—strode from around the left corner of the house. His work boots crunched on the gravel edging the driveway with a steady, purposeful rhythm.

He was taller than me by a couple of inches, maybe six-two to my five-eleven, and broad-shouldered in a way that suggested time in the gym. He wore denim overalls and a crisp blue work shirt.

A black baseball cap with the word *Winning* embroidered on the front in bright yellow letters sat at a precise angle on his head.

Based on his looks alone, I could see how this guy could successfully con just about anyone. Marilyn didn't have a chance.

I straightened my posture, adding what little height I could, and worked to keep my voice steady. "I'm Mitch."

"I know." His smile was wide, showing perfect white teeth. Not friendly, despite the curve of his lips. "We meet at last."

A prickle of unease crawled up the back of my neck. How much had Jessie told him about me? How much did he know?

He offered his hand, and I should have known it was a mistake to raise mine in kind. Every instinct in my body screamed warning. But refusing a handshake would have shown weakness, would have given him the upper hand before we'd even begun whatever this was.

His hands were enormous. Twice the size of mine, it seemed, with thick fingers and knuckles like small mountains. I braced myself as our palms connected.

He squeezed.

The pressure was immediate and brutal. My knuckles compressed against each other with a grinding sensation that shot straight up my arm. I heard the joints pop—a sound like bubble wrap being crushed—and felt something in my hand shift in a way that shouldn't have been possible.

I tried to hide my grimace, clenching my jaw. Tried to squeeze back, to match his pressure, but it was like trying to crush granite.

Finally, after what felt like an eternity but was probably only three seconds, I pulled my hand away. My fingers tingled, half-numb. I resisted the urge to shake out the pain, to cradle my throbbing hand against my chest.

Lance grinned at me. He had big, ultra-white teeth, and it was a hard grin that said, *Yeah, I meant to do that, bro.*

I cleared my throat, forcing words past the tightness in my throat. "The house is looking good."

"Of course it is." Lance's chest puffed out slightly, his shoulders squaring. "That's what I do. I'm a professional." He tilted his head, studying me with those flat yet strangely intense eyes. They were unsettling, like he could see through my skin to the bones beneath. "Are you taking out my girl on a lunch date?"

I blinked. *My girl?* "Excuse me?"

"She's a heartbreaker, that one." Lance's grin widened, but his eyes stayed cold. Calculating. "I learned that a year ago with her. What do they call it?" He snapped his fingers, like he was searching for a term. "Yo-yo love? She'll string you along, bro—look at how you've come back like a puppy desperate for a treat."

I felt heat flush my chest. The rational part of my brain told me to stay calm, to not let him see he'd gotten to me. But the primitive part, the part that still loved Jessie and felt protective of her, wanted to wipe that smug grin off his face.

"We got divorced only a month ago." I heard my voice rising. "What're you talking about, man? You learned *what* a year ago?"

The front door opened. I saw anger flash across Jessie's face as she regarded Lance standing there beside me in the driveway. Her eyes were narrow, her jaw set in that way I recognized from a thousand arguments during our marriage. She looked ready to kill someone.

"Mitch, come inside with me, please." Her voice was taut, controlled. The kind of control that came from holding back something much bigger. "Now."

Lance whistled a low tune, a mocking sound that might have been the opening bars of "Taps"—the funeral song. "Good luck, bro."

I followed Jessie inside. She shut the door behind me with more force than necessary.

"How long have you really known Lance?" The question came out harsher than I'd intended. "Tell me the truth, Jessie."

"Unbelievable." She crossed her arms over her chest, a defensive posture I knew well. "What did he tell you?"

"He called you a heartbreaker, said he learned that a year ago. But you told me that before you hired him, you hadn't seen him since high school. Was that true?"

She pressed her hands to her temples, her eyes squeezing shut for a beat. Her shoulders rose and fell with a deep breath. When she opened her eyes again, they were like steel—hard, determined, and showing the strength that had first attracted me to her all those years ago.

"This is what this man does, Mitch," she said in a soft but steady voice. "This is what I've been living with for the past few weeks. Mom and I can barely talk without coming to an argument, thanks to him."

"He's lying?" I asked.

She gave me a level gaze. Didn't flinch. Didn't look away.

"Of course he is," I said, answering my own question. I pinched the bridge of my nose. "My God, he's smooth. I didn't catch a single hint of deception."

"We need to stay focused." She picked up a manila folder from a nearby table. "Let's go get Mom so we can get this over with."

I nodded, flexing my still-aching hand. The bones protested, a dull throb that matched my heartbeat.

As we moved deeper into the house, I couldn't shake the feeling that we were walking into something much bigger and more dangerous than a simple confrontation about a handyman who'd overstayed his welcome. Whatever game Cutler was playing, we were already several moves behind.

And he knew it.

36: JESSICA

"Mitch!" Mom cried.

The word rang out across the garden, startling a robin from a nearby crepe myrtle. Mom dropped her trowel in the dirt and practically raced toward my ex-husband. She threw her arms around him like he'd returned from a war.

My stomach clenched as I watched them embrace, seeing that eager, grateful expression spread across her face. The same desperate thirst for male validation she'd been showing around Lance lately.

I didn't like it, but this time, it suited my purposes just fine.

"I'm so thrilled you're here!" she said, pulling back just enough to glance at me, dirt-stained gardening gloves still on her hands. "My daughter didn't tell me you were coming!"

"It's great seeing you, too, Marilyn," Mitch said. He met my gaze over Mom's shoulder, and I saw the same grim determination coiled in my own chest reflected back at me. He nodded toward me, a subtle gesture of solidarity.

"It was meant to be a surprise," I said. "Let's go inside and chat."

"Yes, let's do that!" Mom playfully swatted Mitch's shoulder with her gardening glove, leaving a smudge of dirt on his jacket.

"Are you kids reconciling? That's it, isn't it? You're working it out!"

Mitch glanced at me and stammered, his ears reddening the way they always did when he was uncomfortable. "Well . . ."

"Inside, Mom." I gently took her elbow and steered her inside the house.

As we gathered in the living room, my heart kicked into a faster rhythm. I felt it pounding in my ears. "Mom, can you ask Lance to come inside, too?"

Her eyes tightened, the skin at the corners crinkling with confusion and—I saw it clearly now—a flash of defensive protectiveness. For *him*. "What for? This is about you and Mitch. Isn't it?"

My jaw ached. I realized I'd been clenching it. I forced myself to relax, to breathe.

"Lance needs to hear this," I said. "It's important."

Frowning—her lips pressed into that thin, disapproving line I'd seen a thousand times—she went out via the front door. I heard her call out, bright and apologetic: "Lance? Can you come in for a minute, honey?"

Honey?

I sank onto the sofa, and Mitch settled next to me. I flipped open the folder I'd placed on the coffee table, the documents stacked neatly. My evidence.

I had the remote control for the TV close at hand, too. My final card to play.

"Are you sure about this, Jessie?" Mitch asked, his voice barely above a whisper. His knee bounced slightly—a nervous tic I remembered from our marriage.

"I've never been more certain about anything."

Mom filed back inside, Lance trailing behind her. He shut the door and peeled off his work gloves with slow, deliberate movements. I watched his hands—those hands that had invaded my privacy, touched my things, made my life miserable for the past few weeks.

"I'm only forty percent complete with my exterior painting for the day," Lance said, his voice flat and controlled. "I hope this is important. I need to stay on schedule."

Of course he does. God forbid anything interrupt his schemes.

"I'm sorry for the interruption to your day," Mom said, shooting me a look that said I'd better have a good reason for this. "She won't tell me why she's bothering you."

"Have a seat, everyone," I said. "Make yourselves comfortable."

Mom eased into her usual chair, the one with the perfect view of the television. Lance swept his gaze around the room, his attention touching on the documents I'd gathered on the table. I watched his eyes—watched for any flicker of recognition, any crack in that smooth facade. Nothing.

"I'll stand, thank you." He flashed a brief, insincere smile.

"Then let's get to it." I lifted the top page from the stack. My mouth had gone dry. I swallowed again, forced the words out. "So, Lance, tell us: Are you familiar with a company called Legacy Holdings, LLC?"

"Should I be?" Lance said in a flat tone.

Mitch shifted beside me, grumbled under his breath. In the corner of my eye, I saw Mom scowl.

I kept my attention fixed on Lance. He met my gaze without a single indication of guilt or discomfort. He was the smoothest liar I'd ever seen in my life.

But I've got you now. I've finally got you.

"The same day I contacted you through HandyHelper for the very first time," I said, "Legacy Holdings ran a soft inquiry on my credit. I'd never heard of them, never applied for anything that would authorize this company to check my finances. Guess what, Lance? This company ran a soft check on my mother, too, on that very same day."

"Jessie," Mom said, "what is—"

My heart was pounding so hard now I felt dizzy, but I couldn't stop. Not now. "Lance, you were very savvy in how you set up this company. You organized it in Wyoming, where state law allows owners to remain anonymous. Your name isn't tied to the LLC anywhere—you're even using a separate firm as the registered agent. It's the perfect shell organization."

"It sounds like it may be," Lance said. "Unfortunately, I know nothing whatsoever about it, Jessica. Wyoming allows that sort of thing, hmm? I've never been to Wyoming, but I've heard good things —great place if you love the outdoors." He grinned.

You smug jerk. You won't be smiling by the time I'm done.

Beside me, Mitch was shaking his head.

"You didn't have to travel there to take advantage of their business laws," I said. "You could have done it all online. There are companies who specialize in setting up firms anywhere in the world."

"I operate as a sole proprietorship." Lance shrugged, nonchalant. "I'm only a handyman, Jessica. Wow, what are you accusing me of *this* time?"

"I'd like to know that myself," Mom said, her voice sharp with irritation. "What is the point of this inquisition, Jessie? Lance has work to do."

Of course she's defending him. Of course.

"You've compiled an impressive list of residential properties, *bro.*" Mitch leaned forward on the couch and selected a sheet of paper from the gathered documents. His voice carried that professional authority I'd heard him use whenever he discussed business matters. "Who am I, Lance? I'm only a senior fraud investigator for one of the largest credit reporting agencies in the nation. In the past ten years or so, Legacy Holdings has acquired a portfolio of homes— many of which appear to have once belonged to your satisfied clients."

Lance said nothing. His eyes held that bottomless look that I had begun to recognize.

But I pushed on. My hands weren't shaking anymore. I felt strangely calm now, riding the adrenaline like a wave.

"We cross-referenced the names of the former owners to women who posted reviews for you on HandyHelper," I said. I passed a couple of pages to my mother that clearly pointed out the connections: It included screenshots of the rave reviews from the HandyHelper app and listings of former homeowner addresses, including their names.

Mom adjusted her glasses as she reviewed the documents. I watched her confusion shift to concentration.

"Dorothy L.," I said, reciting names from memory; I'd reviewed the list over a dozen times. "She's right here in Newnan—her full name is Dorothy Langston. So is Susan B.—her name is Susan Barnes. Patricia W., in Fayetteville, full name Patricia Walker. They had such wonderful remarks about you on the handyman app—before you conned them out of their homes."

"I remember all of them as such lovely clients," Lance said with a sad shake of his head. "I had no clue they'd sold their homes to this company you mention. Legal Holdings is it?"

Still playing dumb. Still lying.

"*Legacy* Holdings, LLC," Mitch said. "And it's highly unlikely that they *sold* their homes. More likely is that you manipulated them into deeding the properties to you."

"I don't understand how anything like that would even work," Lance said with a soft chuckle. He turned to my mother. "Marilyn, have I ever mentioned any such thing to you? Ever?"

Mom glanced up from the documents I'd given her, her mouth drawn into a tight-lipped expression. I held my breath. This was it. This was the moment everything could either fall apart or finally come together.

"No, but I must say, I'm deeply troubled by this, Lance," she said, and I felt something loosen in my chest. She looked at him over the edge of her lenses. "You've admitted these ladies were clients of yours. They sold or deeded their homes to this company you say you've never heard of, yet the very day Jessie initially hired you, this same company checked our credit without our permission." She shook her head. "No, sir. This smells positively rotten."

I could have hugged Mom then.

"I'm a simple handyman," Lance said calmly, but I heard the slight edge creeping into his voice. He looked at each of us, in turn. "I fix things, and I'm fantastic at what I do. But that's all I do, friends. You've created this bizarre conspiracy around me—shell companies in Wyoming, bilking beloved clients out of their homes—and I truly find it laughable and downright offensive."

"He claims he's a simple handyman, operating as a sole proprietorship," I said, reaching for another sheet. I passed it to Mom; it was a VIN ownership report, available online for a nominal fee. "Yet his van is owned by a commercial entity according to the vehicle records. The details of that company are private, but he's obviously lying about being this basic handyman doing business as plain ole Lance Cutler."

"It's a leased vehicle," Lance said. "Is that a crime now?"

"The vehicle was purchased a month after Legacy Holdings was formed in Wyoming," Mitch said. "Coincidence, huh?"

"My goodness," Mom said, putting her hand to her head.

"I don't know anything about that," Lance said, but his voice sounded hollow now. Empty.

I picked up the remote control and turned on the TV.

"Even if everything we're accusing you of has nothing to do with you," I said, meeting his gaze, "would you care to explain why you were trespassing in my locked bedroom?"

I pressed a button. The nanny cam footage played on the big screen in full color, with perfect clarity. Lance entering my room. Lance pocketing a key. Lance opening my drawers, carefully rifling through my things. Lance reviewing legal pads where I'd written notes. Lance adjusting framed photos, tilting them just enough—just enough to make me wonder if I was going mad.

Watching this, Mom gasped.

"This is a deepfake video, generated by AI," Lance said, but I heard the desperation in his voice. For once, I'd rattled him. He flicked his hand toward the screen dismissively. "AI can create video of anything, Marilyn. Jessica is so desperate to get rid of me she used AI to create this fake footage."

Mitch laughed. "Man, you sound ridiculous now. Seriously."

"At first, I couldn't figure out *how* you got past my locked door, since only I had the keys," I said. "Then I did a little research and learned about something called key impressioning. It allows you to basically make your own key from a lock. It takes time and only a trained locksmith would know how to do it—but you happen to offer locksmithing services, don't you, Lance? Part of your Family Care Package, is it?"

I smiled at him. Lance only gave me that empty look. But I saw it for what it really was—not emptiness, but calculation. The look of a predator caught in a trap, evaluating his options.

"I've heard enough," Mom said, her voice cutting through the tension. She glanced at the TV with a disgusted twist of her lips. "And frankly, I've seen enough." She placed the papers on a nearby table with a decisive thump. "Lance, I'm asking you to leave my home. I no longer want you here, for any reason. Please collect your things and go."

A wave of relief flooded through me so powerfully that my muscles went weak. On shaky legs, I got off the sofa and hugged Mom, and she squeezed me back—hard, the way she used to hug me when I was little and scared.

"I'm sorry I doubted you, baby," she whispered against my hair.

I kissed her cheek, tasting the salt of tears—hers or mine, I couldn't tell.

"Thank you, Mama."

37: JESSICA

Part of the reason why I'd wanted Mitch there was to serve as backup—pure muscle—once I laid out my case against Lance. I had no idea how the man would react to my mountain of proof, evidence I knew he couldn't lie his way out of.

I couldn't stop thinking about his former sister-in-law, Ingrid. Recovering from a horrible, mystery accident after Lance presumably found out I had visited her.

Once we cornered Lance, would he turn violent? Would that calm mask finally crack to reveal what lurked beneath?

When Mom finally ordered him to leave, her voice trembling but determined, I'd braced myself for the explosion. I'd expected Lance to protest, to argue his innocence with that infuriating certainty he wore like a cape. I'd imagined him debating his side with twisted logic, accusing me again of fabricating evidence, of being paranoid. Of letting my imagination run wild, as he'd said so many times before. I'd even prepared myself for threats, for some physical demonstration of the control he'd wielded over our household for weeks.

But all he did was walk out and shut the door behind him, without so much as a comment or a backward glance.

In his sudden absence, the silence in the room felt thick as wool. I felt my heartbeat finally slowing to a normal pace, and I unclenched my clammy hands.

"So . . . that's it?" Mitch said. He'd also risen to his feet when I'd hugged Mom. "He's going to leave without a fuss?"

"I don't want any trouble," Mom said. With effort, she got up; I offered my arm so she could lean on me. The encounter seemed to have drained her. "I'd prefer he leave peacefully. We'll find someone else to finish the house painting."

I stepped to the front window and parted the curtains. Lance's van still occupied the driveway, the rear doors closed. Was he gathering his equipment before he opened the van, stored everything inside, and drove off?

I turned away from the window but gnawed on my bottom lip. Something didn't feel right to me. Lance had walked out too easily, too quietly. This wasn't how his story ended. Men like him—men who'd spent weeks establishing their control, ingraining their presence into every corner of your life—didn't just walk away when confronted.

But I said, "We'll need to change the code on these smart locks he installed, and assign a new PIN for the alarm system. Like, today."

"Of course," Mom said. "I'm still reeling from these revelations, but do whatever makes you feel better, honey."

"It would," I said. "He has no business ever coming back here, but just in case."

"Good idea," Mitch said.

"Are you two reconciling?" Mom's gaze alternated between us, and despite everything that had just happened, a smile touched her lips—that hopeful expression I'd seen so many times since our divorce.

She wouldn't let that go, would she? Not even now, in the aftermath of exposing Lance's manipulation.

"Mitch is here as a supportive friend, nothing more," I said, keeping my voice even despite the irritation flaring in my chest.

"But this is a promising start, yes?" Hope glimmered in her eyes.

I ignored her and pivoted back to the front window, unable to resist checking again. My gut clenched, a physical sensation like a fist squeezing my intestines.

"Guys," I said, "he's still here. I don't think he's leaving."

"But I asked him to go," Mom said. "Maybe he's only gathering his materials. Give him a few minutes."

"I'll check it out." Mitch opened the front door.

I followed him outside. We found Lance on the side of the house, standing on a tall aluminum ladder propped against the wall.

He was painting, using a roller. Whistling as he worked. As if the discussion we'd just had, had never taken place.

Mitch looked at me, and I could read his thoughts as if they were my own: *Can you believe this guy?*

The surreal quality of the moment made me feel unmoored, like I'd slid into some alternate reality where normal rules didn't apply. My heart, which had just started to calm, began hammering again.

Mitch loudly cleared his throat, the sound harsh and deliberate. Lance continued his smooth paint strokes, the roller making soft, rhythmic sounds against the siding.

"Mr. Cutler," Mitch said. "The owner of this residence explicitly asked you to leave immediately. You're trespassing now."

"I'll call the police." I raised my phone and shook it like a weapon.

Lance whistled and painted. I thought he might be wearing earbuds that drowned out our words, but as I stepped closer, peering up at him, my hand positioned to block the sun from blinding me, it was clear that he didn't have anything in his ears.

He was simply ignoring us. Brazenly.

The realization sent a chill through me. This was a power play, I understood suddenly. By continuing to work, by refusing to even acknowledge our presence, he was demonstrating that our confrontation had changed nothing. That he still held control.

"Lance Cutler!" Mitch shouted, hands around his mouth to

form a megaphone. The veins in his neck stood out with the effort. "Get out of here, man! Do you want Jessie to call the cops?"

Lance painted. Whistled. The sound was maddening, each note like a blade pricking at my already frayed nerves.

Shaking his head, Mitch swiveled to me. Sweat glimmered on his forehead. "What's the matter with this guy?"

"I'm calling the police now!" I said.

Whistling, Lance continued to paint. The roller moved up, down, up, down. Steady, with robotic rhythm.

My hands shook as I unlocked my phone. I connected with a 911 dispatcher immediately, and the woman's calm, professional voice provided an anchor in the spiraling chaos of my thoughts.

I didn't describe Lance as a handyman—to my own ears, that sounded ludicrous—but as a "guest who refused to leave." I gave his full name, but I couldn't provide his address. Despite all my detective work, that crucial piece of information had eluded me.

"Has this Lance Cutler threatened anyone at the property?" the dispatcher asked.

"No. But he won't leave. My mom has asked him to leave; *we've* asked him to leave. But he's ignoring us."

"Are you in fear for your safety?"

Was I? The question made me pause. Lance hadn't threatened us, hadn't made any aggressive moves. He was just . . . painting. Being aggressively normal.

"He's trespassing!" I said. "He's out here painting the house like nothing happened, and we've told him he needs to leave immediately. He—"

"He's *painting the house*, ma'am?"

Why had I said that? I heard a new note of skepticism in the dispatcher's voice, that subtle shift in tone that suggested she was questioning whether this was a legitimate emergency or some kind of neighborhood dispute blown out of proportion. Would she dismiss me as a prank caller now? As some hysterical woman who couldn't navigate an awkward social situation?

The scenario sounded absurd when spoken aloud: a man painting a house, refusing to leave. Like something from a dark comedy rather than a genuine threat.

"He might hurt someone," I said, my words tumbling out. "He's got a history of violence. Please send help immediately."

Mitch glanced at me with a quizzical expression. I might have been stretching the truth—I had no tangible evidence that Lance had hurt anyone—but I needed the authorities to take me seriously.

"Ma'am, I'll dispatch a unit," the dispatcher said, her tone still professional but slightly warmer now. "If he's outdoors as you said, I need you to go inside the house and lock the doors. Don't let him inside under any circumstances. An officer will be there as soon as possible."

As the dispatcher terminated the call, Lance began descending the ladder. The aluminum made small creaking sounds as he climbed down. My heart boomed. I retreated several yards instinctively, nearly stumbling over my own feet, and Mitch moved with me, positioning himself slightly between me and Lance.

"The police are on their way," I said. "I warned you."

Lance reached the ground and turned to face us. A slight smile twisted his lips—not friendly, but knowing. Amused, even.

"A history of violence, hmm?" Lance said. "That's quite creative, Jessica."

"I know what you did to Ingrid. The car accident you somehow set up. Do I need to tell the cops about that?"

But I should have learned by then that accusations without heavy proof wouldn't provoke a response from him. He'd mastered the art of making you doubt your own perceptions.

"I haven't seen my beloved Ingrid in years, Jessica. You're imagining things again." His tone was conversational, pleasant. With practiced efficiency, he collapsed the ladder, the metal clanging loudly in the afternoon. "No wonder you couldn't sustain your marriage. I feel sorry for you, Mitch, and what you had to put up with from this paranoid drama queen."

"Just go, man," Mitch said.

"My work here isn't done." Lance easily hefted the ladder across one broad shoulder. "I always finish the job. Always. Remember that."

He clicked his tongue and toted the ladder back to his van, walking with unhurried steps.

By the time the police arrived fifteen minutes later, their cruiser rolling up with lights flashing but no sirens, Lance was long gone. The officer took my statement with that particular brand of police skepticism reserved for domestic disputes and neighbor quarrels. He wrote everything down in his notebook, but I could see in his eyes that he thought we were overreacting.

"If he comes back, call us immediately," the cop said, handing me a card. "We'll have this incident on file."

But something told me—some cold certainty that had settled like ice in my bones—that we hadn't seen the last of Lance Cutler. Not by a long shot.

38: JESSICA

"It sounds like you nailed this jerk, once and for all." Claire's face filled my iPhone screen, her expression a mix of satisfaction and concern. "Good for you, girl. You'll never see him again if he knows what's good for him."

Holding the phone, I paced the carpet in my bedroom. Through the window, late afternoon sunlight slanted across the floor in golden bands. Hours had passed since I'd confronted Lance, but my body hadn't gotten the memo—I felt jittery and couldn't keep still.

Mitch had driven back to Dunwoody. Mom had repeatedly insisted that he stay for an early dinner, promising to cook her excellent smothered chicken, a dish she knew we both loved. To his credit, Mitch had declined with genuine regret in his voice, and when we parted, I could tell he didn't want to go.

I was grateful for Mitch's help, but I wasn't sure when—or if—I would see him again. We weren't partners, and I didn't consider him a friend, either: He was an accomplice in my plan, nothing more. Romance wasn't always the final objective, no matter what the Hollywood movies promised.

"Lance told us he always finishes the job," I said, stopping mid-pace. I caught my reflection in the dresser mirror—my hair disheveled, eyes tinged with red. I looked like I'd been in a fight. Maybe I had been. "It sounded like a threat."

Claire's image on the screen shifted as she adjusted her position. "If he shows up again, warn him you'll call the police—and do it. He'll be terrified of having an arrest on his record. For someone in his line of work, it would tank his business. HandyHelper runs criminal background checks, and I'm pretty sure they monitor their contractors on an ongoing basis."

The tension in my shoulders ebbed a fraction. "Excellent point."

"He's gone for good, Jess." Claire's smile was meant to be reassuring, but I caught a faint flicker of uncertainty in her eyes. "Relax. Celebrate with a glass of wine and a good night's sleep. You've earned both."

"Both of which sound wonderful." Sighing, I sat on my desk chair, springs creaking beneath my weight. "Now, I need to hire someone else to finish painting the house. It's about half-done. I promised Mom I'd take care of it."

"Don't hire them from HandyHelper this time." Claire laughed.

"I heard that." I laughed, too. "But you know what bugs me? Mom and I avoided being victims of this guy, but he's not going to give up his scam. He'll move on to the next mark and start his routine all over again. I feel like I need to warn people about him."

"How would you even do that?"

"I could send an email to HandyHelper. I can't edit my review of him, but I could send them the details of what I found out. They could flag him in their system, maybe investigate."

Claire's headshake was immediate. "Let it go, Jess. This guy will eventually get what's coming to him. Karma's real." Her expression softened. "You did what you needed to do. You protected yourself and your mom. That's enough."

Or maybe it's my responsibility, I thought, but didn't say it aloud. Claire had always been a "live and let live" person, the friend who avoided confrontation, who believed the universe would sort things out on its own. She'd never agree, and I was too tired to argue about philosophical differences.

We talked for a few more minutes—Claire's upcoming ski trip in Aspen over the holidays, her husband's new Harley that gave her anxiety whenever he took it out—safe topics that let my heart rate finally begin to slow. When we ended the call, I sat for a moment in the quiet, watching dust motes drift through the slanting sunlight.

My throat felt scratchy. When had I last sipped water? I was on the verge of dehydration. Extreme mental effort could be as taxing as physical exercise.

I found Mom in the kitchen, both hands wrapped around the faucet handle in the double-basin sink, lips pressed together in concentration.

"We've got a slow leak here," she said, her voice carrying that note of defeat that meant one more thing added to an impossibly long list. Water dripped steadily, each drop echoing in the stainless-steel basin with a hollow plink. "It keeps dripping, no matter how tight I turn it."

"Oh. I noticed that."

"Lance was going to address it. It was one of the items on his list, noted in our contract."

"I'll call a plumber in the morning."

"Well . . . okay." Mom frowned, looked as if she wanted to say more, but kept silent.

Was she having second thoughts about kicking Lance out? After everything I'd shown her—the shell company shenanigans, the invasion of privacy, the pattern of lies—was she still missing Lance?

"Whatever needs to get done here, I promise I'll take care of it," I said. "We can make a list of items together. Sound good?"

"Thanks, Jessie." But her voice lacked conviction, her gaze already drifting to the dripping faucet like it represented everything that was breaking down again.

"Also: This contract you signed with Lance. Does it say anything about early termination? Are we going to owe him a ton of money for booting him out of the house?"

Mom touched her chin, her eyes going vacant. "I . . . I don't recall."

"Can I read it? Please?"

I expected her to resist, but in her obvious state of fatigue, she only shrugged and shuffled out of the kitchen, leading me to a small room that had long served as a home office/library. During her teaching career, Mom had spent countless nights locked in here grading student essays in her careful red pen, creating lesson plans on Shakespeare and Faulkner, the desk lamp glaring until midnight.

The oak file cabinet stood in the corner, scarred and solid, a relic from a yard sale. Mom pulled open the second drawer, the hardware emitting a rusty screech; she rooted around for a moment and finally withdrew a manila folder. The corner label, in her impeccable cursive handwriting, read: "Handyman Contract."

She offered it to me. Inside, I found a printed, seven-page document, laying out the terms between the "Contractor" identified as Lance Cutler, of 217 Shady Oaks Lane, in Newnan, and the "Client" with my mom's name and home address.

"I never knew where he lives," I said.

"You could have asked me. It's plainly stated there. He's on the southern outskirts of town."

I scanned the agreement. The contract detailed the "Family Care Package" tasks in surprisingly comprehensive fashion—each job itemized, materials specified, timelines noted. It looked professional.

I found a paragraph about allowing access to the house that only stated, "Client will ensure Contractor has necessary access to Property to complete all agreed-upon Work." It stated nothing about Lance showing up at three o'clock in the morning to switch on a power drill, but the statement was broad enough for his actions to be covered in the contract.

I located the termination clause on page four. The language was straightforward, almost disappointingly so: "Within thirty days of termination, client will render full payment for all services in progress or completed."

"This seems fairly straightforward." I thumbed through the pages again, looking for hidden clauses, gotcha language, anything that would give Lance leverage. But the agreement was . . . simple. Basic. Not the document of a sophisticated con artist. "Nothing about penalties or fees for early termination."

For a scammer, it was suspiciously clean. But maybe that was part of the con, too—gain trust through apparent transparency, present yourself as reasonable and straightforward while you slowly tightened the noose in other ways. The constant check-ins, the manipulation, the emotional control—none of that would show up in a contract.

"Are you satisfied now?" Mom said. "I should owe him for the paint supplies and the work he did today, but otherwise I'm paid in full. I'll send him a check in the mail for the balance. We don't need to see him again, if that concerns you."

"Good. I can stop locking my door."

Mom pressed her lips together in a grim expression. "I'm upset about his invasion of your privacy, and the other things . . ." She sighed. "But it *was* nice to have him around each day, performing repairs and improvements. He was excellent at his trade, whatever else you want to say about him."

"We don't need him, Mom. I'll take care of everything. I'll either do it myself or hire someone safe and legitimate. Trust me, okay?"

Mom looked at me, silent for a long moment. "All right."

Later that night, an alarm went off.

39: JESSICA

It sounded like an emergency siren.

The noise ripped me out of my first restful slumber in weeks. The siren's wail was a solid wall of noise that pressed against my eardrums and vibrated through the mattress springs. It seemed to emanate from directly below my room, from the bowels of the house itself, as if the building were screaming in pain.

Someone tripped the security alarm.

I felt my throat tighten. Lance's face flashed in my mind: the empty eyes and artificial smile, promising, *I always finish the job.*

The room was dark, the door shut. I groped for my phone on the nightstand, but in my general state of disorientation, I fumbled it. I heard it thud onto the carpet with a muffled thump that I felt more than heard over the siren's cacophony.

Cursing, I flung aside the tangled bedsheets and swung my legs to the side of the mattress.

The bedroom door flew open.

A scream surged to my lips, but in the sudden burst of dim hallway light I recognized Mom's silhouette: her thin frame, her shoulders hunched, her white nightgown ghostly in the dimness. She rushed into my room, moving faster than I'd seen her move in ages, and huddled beside me like a frightened child.

I switched on the bedside lamp, blinked against the sudden glare.

Mom clutched something in her hands. It took my sleep-fogged, panic-addled brain several seconds to recognize the dark metal shape: a revolver.

I didn't realize she had a gun. It must have been Dad's. Seeing it now, in Mom's shaking hands, her finger hovering too close to the trigger, sent a fresh bolt of terror through my chest.

"Jessie . . . someone's broken into the house," she whispered. Her breath was hot, her mouth only a few inches from my face, but the whooping alarm was so loud I strained to hear her.

"Lemme get my phone," I said. My voice came out steadier than I felt, though my hands still shook. I placed my palm over the firearm, gently moving it away from my direction. "Be careful with the gun, Mom. Please."

Shivering, Mom nodded. I picked up my phone; it lay on the floor beside one of the bed's wooden legs.

The time read 2:28 AM.

The witching hour. The time when bad things happened in horror stories.

I opened the security alarm app with clumsy fingers, praying for information, for context, for anything that would explain the hellish noise still screaming through the house.

The screen loaded. Bold, blinking letters declared: *System Test Executing.*

Some of the tension eased out of me.

"It's only a test." I showed Mom the phone.

Mom's brow crinkled, deep furrows appearing between her eyebrows. She looked from the phone to me and back again, disbelief etched across her features. "Are you certain? Who would test the system at this hour?"

Lance, I almost said. But I couldn't say it, not again. Because he was gone now. Right?

I pressed the button to end the test. The siren spiraled into silence. In the aftermath, I felt my ears still ringing, and my own heartbeat seemed to be the loudest thing in the room.

In the app, I checked the security cameras. Both were online. The back-door camera hadn't detected any motion since it tracked Mom outside earlier in the afternoon; the front showed only that a stray black cat, an animal I'd seen before, had crossed the sidewalk two hours ago, which would not have triggered anything. Front and rear entryways were shut, secure.

"No one's here," I said. "It's only us."

"Why did the alarm go off?" Mom asked.

She was still holding the gun, and I gently reached to take it from her. I placed it on my bed.

"Someone triggered the system test," I said. "Or it was a glitch. The monitoring company hasn't called us, which is what usually happens when you test these things."

Mom didn't look reassured. "We should go check the house, to be sure."

I knew immediately that "we" really meant "me." Mom would wait here, in the relative safety of my bedroom, while I ventured downstairs to confront whatever might be lurking in the shadows.

"I'll go take a look," I said.

"Take this." She reached for the handgun.

"No, you keep that with you. Put it somewhere safe," I said. "I didn't know you even had a gun, but that's a separate discussion we can have later. I'll be right back."

"Be careful."

Phone in hand, I left the bedroom, Mom standing beside the bed. I quickly checked upstairs, found nothing out of place, and descended the staircase, switching on lights when I reached the bottom, setting the first floor ablaze with brightness.

The control panel for the alarm, which Lance had installed in the first-floor hallway near the door, declared: "Ready to Arm."

The front door was locked—I tested the handle twice, yanking it hard enough to rattle the frame. The dead bolt held firm. Through the sidelight window, I could see our driveway bathed in moonlight, the trees beyond swaying in a light breeze. No cars except ours. No shadowy figures.

No Lance.

The back door, when I checked it, was also locked. I walked around the first floor, testing every window latch, peering out into the darkness beyond each pane of glass. The house was sealed tight. In the garage, I found only the usual chaos.

I circled back to the control panel.

"Is everything okay?" Mom asked from the top of the staircase.

"All clear," I said. "You can go back to bed."

As she shuffled to her room, I turned back to the alarm system's glowing digital display.

Earlier that day, after we kicked Lance out, I had changed the access PIN. It had taken me twenty minutes to navigate the overly complex menu system, but I'd done it. Changed the four-digit code from the one he'd set up to something only Mom and I knew. I'd tested it twice to make sure it worked.

That meant Lance could not have remotely triggered a system test. He couldn't access the system at all anymore, couldn't control it from his phone or his van or wherever he spent his evenings doing God knows what.

Unless he'd created a back door into the system: administrator override codes I didn't know about.

"No, it was just a glitch," I said aloud to the empty hallway, testing the words, seeing if they felt true.

They didn't.

But I was so tired of suspecting him, of assuming his hand was at work in every bad thing. Maybe I was losing my mind. Maybe weeks of stress and paranoia had finally broken something in my brain.

I pressed the button to arm the system—hadn't I done that earlier, before bed?—and watched the display cycle through its arming sequence. Forty-five seconds until full activation. Time enough to get upstairs before the motion detector kicked in.

But I didn't move. I stood there in the bright hallway, bare feet on cold tile, and let the seconds tick past. A few seconds before it armed, I hurried to the staircase and checked the app on my phone.

Armed—Stay Mode.

From the steps, I stared at it for another full minute, waiting for it to do something unexpected, to prove my paranoia justified.

It did nothing. Armed and ready like usual.

Finally, I turned and trudged to my room. My legs felt heavy, my whole body weighted down with exhaustion and adrenaline crash.

It took me a long time to get back to sleep. My eyes kept snapping open at every tiny sound: the house settling, the air conditioner clicking on, a tree branch scraping against the siding. My spidey sense tingled, that little voice in the back of my head that was rarely wrong.

Something was going on here.

But what?

40: JESSICA

On Friday morning, two days after we had fired Lance, I drove downtown to Main Street to meet a new prospective marketing client: Coweta Hardware, a business that offered home improvement items and had been a Newnan staple for decades, despite the rise of big-box stores like The Home Depot and Lowe's—the kind of local spot where loyal customers paid with cash and dropped in just to chat with staff. They had a brick storefront just off the town square and were on my targeted prospects list.

Only a few days ago, I'd confirmed my meeting with the store manager, a gentleman named Mr. Clyde Johnson. He had sounded genuinely interested, even eager.

I expected an easy sale.

The hardware store's front window displayed a rotating fan, garden hoses coiled like sleeping snakes, and a handwritten sign advertising a sale on leaf blowers. A bell jangled overhead as I pushed through the door.

I approached the front counter where a college-age girl with red-dyed hair was scrolling through her phone.

"Good morning," I said, injecting warmth into my voice. "I have a ten o'clock appointment with Mr. Johnson."

She glanced up, nodded, and called toward the back office. "Grandpa? Your appointment's here."

My pulse quickened—that familiar pre-meeting adrenaline. I shifted my tote bag to my other shoulder, preparing my smile, my opening line about how much I admired businesses that had staying power in today's market.

The office door opened. A slender, sixty-something man emerged wearing cowboy boots that clicked against the linoleum, jeans, and a red uniform vest over a white button-down shirt. He wore wire-rimmed glasses perched on his narrow nose. His thinning white hair was neatly combed back.

But he wore a scowl so deep that I felt my heart thud.

Something's wrong.

I gave my best smile and a cheerful greeting. "Good morning, I'm—"

"We won't be needing your services, Miss Taylor," Mr. Johnson said. His voice dripped with that slow, syrupy Georgia drawl that could make even rejection sound almost polite. Almost. "We've been doing fine with things the way they've been. Got plenty of loyal folks that's been coming in for years."

My smile faltered. "Sir, you sounded very interested when we spoke on Monday. May I ask why the change of mind?"

"Thought it over some more. Social media whatever isn't what our business needs right now, ma'am."

"But we discussed this exact thing. You said you wanted to promote your social media pages to draw in new customers."

He glared at me over the edge of his glasses, and I saw something in his eyes that went beyond simple disinterest. It was contempt.

"I *know* what I said, ma'am. Now, I'm saying we don't need it. Is that clear?"

My spine stiffened. The tote felt suddenly heavy, dead weight pulling at my shoulder. This wasn't just a prospect changing his mind. This was personal. This was the first time someone had looked at me like I was nothing—like I was less than nothing—since I'd started my business.

What had I done to deserve this? I struggled for a response.

"Thanks for your consideration, Mr. Johnson," I said. "But if you should reconsider—"

"My thoughts are settled on the matter." He gestured toward the front door with a pencil he'd been holding, a dismissive flick of his wrist. "Unless you're buying something, ma'am, show yourself out right over there."

The red-haired clerk had watched this entire humiliating exchange, and a customer in the cleaning supplies aisle had stopped browsing and turned toward us. I felt every eye in the store tracking my walk of shame toward the exit.

The bell jangled again as I pushed through the door, and the sound seemed to mock me. I walked to my car on legs that felt unsteady, my vision blurring. I fumbled with my key fob, finally got the door open, and collapsed into the driver's seat.

I sat in my car with my tote bag on my lap and drew in deep breaths.

Big girls don't cry, Jessie. Suck it up.

I pinched the bridge of my nose hard, pressing until it hurt, using the pain to force the tears back. My throat ached with the effort of not sobbing.

This was only business, I told myself. Not personal. If I couldn't handle setbacks without losing my composure, this enterprise of mine was destined to fail. Every successful business owner faced rejection. This was just one prospect, one meeting, one closed door.

But I couldn't rationalize Mr. Johnson's extreme about-face. After speaking to me so warmly on the phone earlier—after asking me questions, taking notes, even mentioning specific pain points his business was facing—he'd transformed into someone who acted like I'd insulted him just by walking into his store.

It didn't make sense.

Move on.

I clutched the steering wheel, drummed my fingers on the faux leather.

But then something shifted in my chest. Not despair.

Anger.

On impulse, I shoved the car door open and left my bag on the seat. I marched back across the sidewalk. The bell jangled as I pushed through the door a second time.

The clerk's eyes went wide. "Ma'am, I don't think—"

I ignored her and headed straight for the bulletin board near the bank of registers. It was the kind of community board you saw in every small-town business: flyers for church socials, business cards for local services, handwritten ads for yard sales and lost cats.

My eyes scanned the cards. Pizza delivery. Housekeeping. Plumbing. Landscaping.

And handymen.

Lance Cutler's card occupied a prominent spot on the board.

My hands shook as I reached up and tore it down. The pushpin clattered to the floor.

"Where is Mr. Johnson?" I asked the clerk.

She made a vague motion toward another section of the store. I found him doing inventory in an aisle full of screws of assorted sizes.

At my return, he scowled again. "What is it now? I was quite clear—"

I showed him Lance's card. "Is Lance Cutler a friend of yours, sir? A longtime customer, huh? Probably gets all his supplies from you?"

Redness rose in his cheeks—which was all the answer I needed. I saw it all—the phone call Lance must have made, the poison he'd dripped into Mr. Johnson's ear, the lies he'd spread about me.

My head pounded.

I had written Coweta Hardware on my list of business prospects. Lance would have seen that list when he snooped inside my bedroom and found my documents; he might have even snapped a photo of it.

"Did Lance tell you not to hire me?" I asked.

Mr. Johnson cleared his throat. "Ma'am, I'm asking you to leave now."

"He's *lying* about me," I said. "This is his revenge because my mom and I fired him from a job. Whatever he told you about me—it's not true."

"I don't know anything about that, but I know I want you out of here." He pulled up his pants. "I'm giving you five seconds. Ma'am."

"He's a con man and a liar, sir." I ripped the business card in half, the sound satisfying in the quiet aisle. "Remember that."

I flung the ripped-up card to the floor and walked out.

41: JESSICA

Rio Nail Lounge was three blocks down the road from Coweta Hardware. My hands trembled on the steering wheel as I drove, the discovery of Lance's sabotage still crackling through my nervous system. Every muscle in my body felt wound tight, coiled springs ready to snap.

But I needed to check on Ingrid.

I felt guilty about what had happened to her. If my theory was right and Lance had gone after her because he learned I'd spoken to her about him, I bore some responsibility. If I hadn't questioned her, she would be healthy and safe, spending her days working with clients in her salon.

And—Lance was coming after me now, too, wasn't he? What if bad-mouthing me to his local business buddies was only the start of his revenge campaign? What if he had more trouble in mind for me?

I always finish the job. Always. Remember that.

I shivered.

Someone might have called me paranoid, but I'd learned to trust my gut instincts with this guy.

The last I'd heard from Ingrid's staff, she was in the hospital, recovering from a mysterious car accident. That was on Monday; today was Friday.

I scored a parking spot in front of the salon and went inside, holding my breath.

But Ingrid's station was still empty.

"Hey there, good morning," Chloe called from behind the front desk. She looked up from her appointment book and recognition flickered across her face. "I remember you. You're Miss Ingrid's client."

"Is she doing better? You told me earlier this week she was in the hospital after a terrible accident."

Chloe's professional smile softened into something bittersweet, tinged with genuine concern. "She's home now, thank God." She exhaled slowly, and I caught the slight sag in her shoulders that suggested she'd been holding that worry close. "But honestly, I don't know when she'll return to work. I can book you with another technician?"

"I'd love to send Ingrid a Get-Well card. Do you have her mailing address?"

"She'd love that. Of course."

Chloe scribbled an address on the back of a salon business card and slid it across the desk to me.

"Thanks so much." I glanced at the card, saw a Newnan street address, and dropped it into my purse.

"About that appointment?" Chloe asked.

"I'll call later to set up a time."

Back in my car, I typed Ingrid's home address into my phone. It was about an eight-minute drive away.

What are you thinking, Jess? You've already gotten this woman into trouble by talking to her the first time.

A gift shop was across the street. There, I picked up a "Get Well Soon" greeting card and came back to my car.

It took me seven minutes to reach her house. Ingrid lived in a quaint neighborhood of charming bungalows with two-car garages, on tidy lawns. A cute, storybook home.

The driveway was empty. If Ingrid suffered an auto wreck that landed her in the hospital, it was likely that her own car was totaled. But she might be inside, recovering.

I parked across the street, in the deep shade of an elm.

I would drop off the card in her mailbox. That was all, I promised myself. I wouldn't knock on her door. I wouldn't ask questions and press for more details about Lance. I would leave the card and be on my way.

As I reached for my door handle, I saw the sectional garage door scroll upward. Red taillights flared in the shadows.

Someone was pulling out of the garage.

I paused with my fingers on the door. A white Chevy Lumina with Arkansas tags backed out and neared the end of the driveway.

I slid down in my seat, but I turned enough to get a good look at the driver's-side profile as she slid on a pair of sunglasses.

"Oh, shit," I said.

It was Melody Rockwell.

Lance's supposedly dead ex-wife.

42: JESSICA

I t couldn't be Melody Rockwell.

The woman had died a decade ago. Her family mourned her passing, posted an obituary in the newspaper, and held a memorial service.

Possibly it was a cousin, some relative who shared a family resemblance. On my father's side, I had a first cousin who looked so much like me, people used to assume we were sisters.

I'd gotten only a brief glance at the driver, a side view before she put on an oversized pair of sunglasses—the style of shades that movie stars donned when they ventured out in public and didn't want to be recognized. Not a long, lingering look.

But when the Chevy had driven halfway down the block, I shifted into Drive and pressed the gas.

"What are you doing, Jess?" I said aloud.

I followed the car, from several vehicle lengths behind. My palms were damp on the steering wheel.

I'd never done anything like this in my life. Was this what it felt like to lose control? Because I felt as though I was on autopilot: My brain wanted one thing, but my body had its own agenda.

Traffic to wherever the driver was headed was light on that late Friday morning. We kept to residential streets for multiple turns. I eased up on the accelerator, so as not to arouse suspicion from my target by following too closely. That was what people did in the movies when they tailed someone, right?

Finally, we reached a red light at a busy intersection. I was two cars behind the Chevy. She made a sudden right, into the flow of traffic.

I cursed under my breath. I was going to lose her.

The traffic signal switched to green. I roared ahead, hung a right —and just ahead, I saw the Chevy swing left, into a strip mall parking lot. A big Kroger supermarket and several smaller retail shops occupied the complex.

I veered into the parking lot as the Chevy pulled into a spot near the grocery store. I didn't want to park too close to her, so I found a slot a couple of rows away, positioning my vehicle to allow a view of the front of the market.

Now what? I drummed the wheel with clammy fingers.

After about a minute, she got out of her car. Whoever she was, she wore a black baseball cap, a pink hoodie, baggy gray sweatpants, and sneakers. The chunky movie-star sunglasses were still in place.

Was that really Melody Rockwell?

I wasn't so sure anymore. Because: Why would Melody Rockwell actually be alive and well and living in Arkansas? Why would she have returned to Newnan?

Possibilities simmered in my thoughts.

I sucked in a deep breath and got out of the car.

It was one of those supersized Kroger stores that sold everything: groceries, clothing, and anything else you might need. Inside the entrance, I pivoted in a semicircle, not seeing the woman, not sure where to even start looking.

"May I help you, ma'am?" an employee asked.

"I'm looking for my sister," I said, surprised how smoothly the lie burst forth. "She just walked in—a lady wearing big sunglasses and a pink hoodie?"

He frowned, thinking, then pointed. "I think I saw her going toward the pharmacy."

"Thanks."

The pharmacy department was on the west side of the store. Over there, I saw her at the prescription Pick Up window.

Was she getting meds for Ingrid?

Slowly, I walked toward her. When I was about ten feet away, I said: "Melody Rockwell?"

If that wasn't her name, she wouldn't have responded, I reasoned. People were attuned to react, reflexively, to hearing their names spoken aloud.

The woman whirled. My stomach did a somersault.

It's her.

Her lips contorted in a grimace, which quickly vanished.

"Who did you say?" she said.

"Melody Rockwell," I said again, and stepped closer. "I thought you passed ten years ago. What's going on?"

"I don't know what you mean." The woman flashed a quick, fake smile. "Sorry, honey. I think you've mistaken me for someone else."

The pharmacist handed the woman a stapled brown-paper bag. She thanked him, and turned, moving away from me.

I followed.

"You're in town to visit your sister, Ingrid," I said. "Her accident brought you out of hiding, didn't it? You've been hiding all these years from *him*, even faked your own death to fool him."

She walked faster, weaving down aisles. I kept pace with her—to anyone watching, we probably looked like two reluctant friends speed-walking through the grocery store.

"Stay away from me," she said over her shoulder. "You sound like a lunatic."

"All I want to know is who I'm dealing with. I already figured out he's a con artist, but I suspect he might be worse than that."

She stopped so suddenly I almost collided with her. She lifted her oversized sunglasses.

I gasped.

Her right eye looked almost real, but I had seen prosthetic ones before. It was a high-quality simulation, closely mimicked her other, real eye, but on a closer look, it didn't track movement, didn't look completely lifelike.

"Did Lance . . . do that to you?" I asked.

"Leave us alone," she whispered. "Please."

"I just want to know—"

"You've no idea what he's capable of. Stay away from him."

"Can you—"

"You've dragged my family back into a nightmare. *Please leave us alone.*"

Melody Rockwell snapped her sunglasses back in place, spun on her heel, and walked away.

This time, I didn't follow her.

43: JESSICA

Over the next week, my marketing consulting business flatlined.

Prospective clients, all of them local companies in my hometown, abruptly backed out of scheduled presentations, just like Coweta Hardware had done. They claimed they were suddenly "not interested" in the services I offered.

But what was worse was the damage to my contracted clients—those who had agreed to a marketing package, signed contracts, remitted payment. They claimed *I* canceled our contracts myself, via email. When I denied I had ever done this and asked for proof, the contacts forwarded me a detailed "termination of services" message sent from a Gmail account that used my business name, JT Consulting; it even included a phone number for them to call with any questions.

The reason given in these fake emails for the "termination" made me sound thoroughly unprofessional: *"Due to serious issues in my personal life, including a traumatic divorce, I've found myself in an unstable emotional state that leaves me unable to complete the necessary duties to fulfill our contract."* Oh, and the cancellation message happened to promise that I'd pay them back in thirty days for whatever sums they had already paid, as an apology for their inconvenience.

But the messages weren't sent from my legitimate company email address and didn't reference my actual phone number. When I called the number myself, it went straight to voicemail, without so much as a greeting.

"I thought I was being careful, writing everything down in my business journal," I said to Claire. "But he used it to destroy my business, and I can't prove it."

It was late on a sunny and cool Saturday afternoon, and we were at Claire's house in Fayetteville, sitting on the back deck sipping skinny margaritas. I was on my third drink, which probably negated the value of it being a "skinny" cocktail. Her husband was going to make carne asada tacos on the grill. Knowing I was reeling from these setbacks, Claire had invited me over.

Their back deck had recently been remodeled and expanded, and it looked fantastic. I noticed her husband had a new SUV, too, a champagne-colored Cadillac Escalade.

It seemed like they were minting money. It was tough to resist a twinge of envy as I struggled to build a basic business for myself.

"You'll recover from this, Jessie," Claire said. "You're resilient. Always have been. You'll bounce back stronger than ever."

"The two clients I convinced to talk to me think I'm trouble," I said. I slurped my drink. "They believe I've got personal issues with a stalker, and they're afraid to do business with me now."

"That's terrible." Claire shook her head. "Did you contact the police? This sounds like some sort of law is being broken."

I nodded. "They weren't helpful. Like I said, I can't *prove* Lance is behind any of this. Anyone can open a Gmail account or buy a burner phone and give out the number. It's almost impossible to trace any of it back to him."

"Are you sure Lance is behind it?" Claire asked with a thoughtful look.

"Seriously?" I stared at her. "Who else would it be?"

"Well . . . you're no friend of the Rockwell sisters, either, these days."

Earlier, I'd told her everything about my encounters with Ingrid and Melody.

"Melody risked a lot, coming back to town to check on her sister," Claire said. "If Lance found out about that, that she's still alive after evidently faking her own death . . ."

"I feel guilty about involving them, but trust me, I'm never reaching out to either of those ladies again. They've suffered enough." I set my drink on the table. "But no, this is all Lance. No one else."

"But you can't prove it."

"He's a scammer, but more than that, he's a psychopath. He's never been arrested, has no criminal record. We've verified that."

"But . . ."

"But he's got blood on his hands. From something. I'm convinced of it."

"Sounds like you're planning to do more digging, Jess. Is that a prudent idea?" Claire folded her arms over her chest, cocked her head as she studied me with an almost clinical look. "Why not just try to find another job in corporate, move on with your life? Until you slip off this guy's radar?"

"You want me to back down? Move on?"

"You said yourself: He's a psychopath. Do you want to tangle more with someone like that? He's a cunning, obviously dangerous man. Is it worth it?"

Was it worth it?

Claire's warning continued to echo in my thoughts when I got back home later that evening.

44: JESSICA

He's a cunning, obviously dangerous man . . .
Although I disagreed with Claire's suggestion that I should move on until I slipped off Lance's radar—give up my business, get a regular company job—I agreed wholeheartedly with her opinion about the threat Lance represented.

He had somehow engineered an accident to land his ex–sister-in-law in the hospital. His ex-wife, after abuse that resulted in a permanently disfigured eye, had divorced him and fled, so terrified she assumed a false identity and her family declared her legally dead.

But Claire's warning raised the question: What if there was more?

If there was, I was going to find it. I wasn't going to sit back and let this guy ruin my life, destroy my ambitions. Already, I had lost almost everything: a well-paying career, a marriage. I wouldn't allow this man to crush my dreams, only because I was afraid of him.

The next morning, Sunday, Mom and I attended church together. She seemed distracted during the drive there and throughout the service, saying little, and I didn't bother asking if she wanted to go to breakfast afterward. I got the sense that she was deep in thought, and I didn't probe.

I was immersed in my own thoughts, too.

When I got home, I hauled out the folder of circumstantial evidence Mitch and I had gathered about Lance.

I ran my finger along the list of names: the women we assumed had deeded their properties to Legacy Holdings, Lance's shell company.

But was that true? Had they voluntarily signed over their homes to him? What, exactly, had happened?

These ladies were more than simple names on a list that I'd compiled to prove a case to my mother. They had lives, legacies.

What if Lance had forced them to go along with his wishes?

I always finish the job . . .

The public records of the property transfers had revealed to us the full names of the unfortunate victims. Using Google, I looked up each of them who had resided in Newnan, one by one . . .

Dorothy Langston.

Susan Barnes.

Patricia Walker.

I found obituaries for all of them. A chill trickled down the back of my neck.

What is going on here?

My fingers blurred across the keyboard.

Cross-referencing their dates of death revealed that they died soon after the property transfers to Legacy Holdings. Within three months.

I sat up straight in my chair, the springs creaking beneath me.

All of them dead within ninety days of selling or deeding their homes to Lance? Was that a coincidence?

Or were their deaths the final item on his punch list?

45: JESSICA

"**I** should have discovered this earlier," Mitch said. "I stopped investigating when I found out these ladies had deeded their properties to Legacy Holdings."

Mitch and I were on the FaceTime call while I sat in my car in the driveway—I didn't want Mom to overhear my conversation. Not only would the topic disturb her, but she would read too much into me having yet another discussion with my ex-husband. *Are you two reconciling, Jessie?*

Reconciliation with Mitch was the furthest thought from my mind. He was the only one with whom I could discuss these things. Claire was my best friend, but I couldn't go along with her suggestion to give up in the hope that Lance would leave me alone.

"Their deaths so soon afterward aren't a coincidence," I said. "Considering how he works, each of them probably, conveniently, suffered some sort of accident, Mitch. That's what my gut tells me."

"Right." Nodding, Mitch stroked his chin. "But gut feelings won't put Cutler in prison."

There it was. That tone. That infuriating, condescending, mansplaining tone that implied I was being emotional and irrational while he was being logical and practical. It had triggered arguments between us more times than I could count, and even now, it still made me clench my jaws.

"I'm aware of that," I said, my voice coming out sharp, but I didn't soften it.

"Without having specific details of how these women died, I don't know what you can do, Jess. Lance was never convicted of a crime. He's got a spotless record."

Of course he does, I thought. *That's the whole point. That's how predators like him operate—they're careful, methodical, patient. They don't leave tracks.*

"Anything else, Captain Obvious?" I said.

Mitch scowled, his face filling more of the screen as he leaned toward his camera. "Save you getting a recorded confession from Lance, I don't see what you can do."

"I could use the obituaries to track down other family members," I said, my mind already working through the logistics. "Chances are, someone has suspicions about Lance. Someone who noticed the coincidences, even if they couldn't prove anything."

Mitch winced as if my suggestion caused him physical pain. His face contorted, eyebrows drawing together, mouth pulling down. "How did that play out with Ingrid Rockwell?"

The question hit me like a smack in the face. Heat flushed my cheeks.

"Excuse me?" I asked, though I'd heard him perfectly.

"Involving innocent family members in these amateur investigations of yours is putting folks at risk."

"Wow, Mitch. And I thought you had turned over a new leaf and were being useful for once."

His jaw tightened. "I don't want anyone else to get hurt. Namely, *you*, babe."

"I can take care of myself. And stop calling me *babe*. Those days are over."

"Sorry. Old habit."

"Have a good evening, Mitch."

"Jess, please, be careful—"

I ended the call and flung the phone onto the passenger seat. Then I snatched it off the seat, scrolled to the Contacts list, and edited Mitch's name from "Cheater" to "Coward."

It was petty. Childish, even. But watching his new contact name appear on my screen sent a hot spark of satisfaction through my chest, warming me from the inside out.

Why had I ever believed I could rely on him? He'd disappointed me before—it was in his DNA to let me down.

Once again, I was on my own.

46: JESSICA

The Newnan Police Department was located in a two-story brick building that could have been copied and pasted from every other government building I'd seen in my life. It was a short drive from the bustling town square.

It was Tuesday, two days after my disappointing call with Mitch. I sat in my car in the parking lot, my tote bag across my lap. I had called the department recently about Lance's business sabotage (a waste of time), but I'd never ventured inside the actual police department, as either a suspect or victim of a crime. How would I describe my reason for visiting without sounding slightly unhinged?

Officer, I'm here as a concerned citizen. I've gathered a ton of research on a con man and potential killer of senior citizens. But, you see, he happens to operate as a handyman.

It was the truth. But it sounded ludicrous.

Still, I had to try.

Before I could talk myself out of it, I hustled out of my car and hurried to the building entrance. A drizzle had begun, cold rain snapping against the pavement, and in my state of distraction I'd forgotten to bring my umbrella.

Inside the vestibule, before I could go any further, a police officer had to process me through a security checkpoint. I dropped my key, purse, and tote onto the conveyor belt, stepped through the scanner, and gathered my belongings on the other side. A big sign directed me toward the police department's reception area.

Several people sat on hard plastic chairs in a small waiting area. A bored-looking officer worked at a desk behind a plexiglass window. Beyond the window, other cops bustled about in a large open office with an air of quiet efficiency. It might have been an insurance company instead of a police department.

The cop at the front desk looked like someone's grandfather: thinning white hair, black-rimmed bifocals, sagging jowls, frail, liver-spotted hands. He typed slowly on a keyboard as I approached, hunting and pecking carefully. His badge read: B. HANDY.

I added my name and time of arrival to a sign-in sheet. The officer didn't look up. I cleared my throat.

"Excuse me, sir," I said. "I'd like to speak to Detective Fields."

I'd located the name of the detective via research. I figured that coming prepared to speak to an actual person would improve my odds of getting results.

"Do you have an appointment, ma'am?" He still didn't look at me; he was cruising on autopilot.

"No, but Detective Fields will be very interested in what I have to share with her," I said.

Officer Handy finally glanced in my direction. His droopy eyebrows lifted.

"What do you have to share with her?" he asked, his voice thick with skepticism.

"A long-running case of systemic business fraud and elder abuse," I said crisply, my rehearsed answer.

"Oh?" Touching his mustache, he nodded slightly. "Have you called us before to report this?"

"Not exactly. It's important that I speak to her. I can give her all the details."

He asked for my contact information. I slid my business card through the slot in the window. He adjusted his bifocals and studied my card.

"You might have to wait a while, ma'am," he said.

"That's no problem. This is important."

Ninety minutes after I'd arrived, the security door opened and a woman strode into the waiting area. She was tall—at least five-ten—and slender, with shoulder-length dark hair pulled into a ponytail, chiseled features, and dark, sharp eyes. She wore a navy-blue sweater, jeans, and scuffed, black leather boots. No uniform, but she moved with the confidence of someone who carried a badge.

"Jessica Taylor?" Her voice was brisk, businesslike.

I stood, grabbing my tote. "Yes. That's me."

"Detective Elana Fields." She didn't offer her hand. "Follow me."

I trailed behind her through the security door and into the warren of cubicles and desks. The main office was louder than it had seemed from the waiting area—phones ringing, conversations overlapping, the clatter of keyboards. The smell of burnt coffee was stronger here, mixed with something else I couldn't quite identify. Sweat, maybe. Stress.

Detective Fields moved fast, weaving through the maze with the ease of long familiarity. I struggled to keep up, my tote bag banging against my hip. Officers glanced at me as I passed, their expressions ranging from curious to indifferent.

She led me to a small office tucked into a corner. It was barely bigger than a closet—gray walls, no windows, a dented metal desk stacked with folders and loose papers, two chairs with worn upholstery. A single photograph stood on the desk that looked like a police academy graduation shot: A younger-looking Detective Fields in uniform, standing with an older woman who had the same sharp cheekbones and dark eyes. Her mother, probably.

She closed the door and settled behind the desk, folding her hands on top of a legal pad.

"Tell me what brings you here, Miss Taylor," she said.

I'd mentally rehearsed my spiel while waiting in the reception area, but being in an actual detective's office, with her keen gaze probing me, triggered a sudden case of lockjaw. *This is real now, Jess. Don't screw it up.*

"Ma'am?" she prompted, her gaze sharpening.

Then it all spilled out of me. As I spoke—to myself, I sounded half-drunk, barely coherent—I dragged my folder out of my tote bag, opened it on her desk, and indicated the documents I'd compiled. The detective plucked the papers out of the folder like a biologist studying specimens.

When I wrapped up, the detective said, "This all sounds very circumstantial, Miss Taylor."

I winced. There was that loathed word again: *circumstantial*.

"But can you investigate?" I asked.

"Based on this footwork of yours?" She indicated the folder with a quick gesture. "It's not enough for a warrant to search Mr. Cutler's home. Not by half."

I felt my shoulders sag. But I asked, "Has anyone else brought a complaint against Lance Cutler? Is there an open investigation, possibly?"

She shrugged. "If there were, I'm not at liberty to share that information with you."

"So, we just have to wait until he kills someone's grandmother again," I blurted.

"I'd suggest you be careful with those accusations."

"Sorry. I've invested so much time in this. I'm frustrated that I can't do anything to stop this guy."

"I'll make a note that we spoke about this matter, but we need more credible evidence for a warrant." The detective rose, indicating that the discussion was over. She passed me her card. "Until then, I'd advise you to leave the investigations to the professionals, ma'am. It's a dangerous world out there."

In other words: *Knock it off.*

"Noted," I said, and tucked her card into my purse.

Her eyes softened. "On a personal note, I'm very close to my mother, too." She glanced at the photograph on her desk. "I can empathize with what's driving you even though I can't take action at this time. Focus your efforts on keeping *her* safe, understand?"

47: JESSICA

I had planned to head home after my fruitless visit to the police department. Instead, after I waited a few minutes in my car for the rainfall to taper off, I drove in the opposite direction of home.

I wanted—*needed*—to see where Lance lived. With my own eyes.

When I discovered his address printed on his contract with my mother, I'd looked it up, of course. Lance had scrubbed the web free of personal details about himself, but the big real estate portals—Zillow, Redfin, Realtor.com, Trulia—each had a listing for his residential address, with photos and property details.

In the pictures, it looked like an unremarkable three-bedroom, two-bath, ranch-style home on the southern outskirts of Newnan. Built thirty-five years ago. Sitting on a wooded one-and-a-half-acre lot. The residence included a basement.

According to online property records, Mr. Eugene Cutler owned the house: Lance's dad, who resided in assisted living, according to Lance.

Ten minutes later, I pulled onto Shady Oaks Lane and reduced my speed. It was a twisty, two-lane country road lined with tall oaks, pines, and elms on both sides, and the blacktop shimmered from the recent rainfall. The last thing I needed was to drive too fast and veer off the road within proximity of his house.

Coming to this area at all was a risk, in fact. What if Lance saw me?

There was no traffic, and the address was just ahead; I saw a black mailbox standing at the end of a driveway. Slowing, I pulled to the shoulder of the road on the opposite side, but in direct view of the drive.

The house stood over a hundred yards away, nestled within a dense grove of trees. A large garage was attached to the house, and I didn't see any vehicles parked in the driveway.

. . . we need more credible evidence for a warrant . . .

I swallowed, my throat dry. My hands tightened on the steering wheel.

Without any doubt, a meticulous man like Lance Cutler kept detailed records in his house of all his business affairs. Proof of his ownership of Legacy Holdings. Information on the properties he had stolen from those poor ladies. Maybe even more. Probably enough to open a criminal investigation and put him away.

I unracked my phone from the dashboard holder, raised it to my window, and snapped several pics of the house. I would add this to my own little investigative trail, though I—

An approaching vehicle grumbled behind me. I glanced in the rearview mirror.

It was a black cargo van with a Mercedes-Benz emblem glistening on the chrome grille.

Cursing, I tossed my phone onto the seat, slammed into Drive, and stomped on the gas pedal. My tires spat up gravel, and the vehicle shimmied dangerously as I veered onto the slick pavement. I clutched the wheel, heart racing, and focused on regaining control of the car.

Ah, I see you ran off the road near my house and hit a tree, Jessica. Would you like some roadside assistance? I can fix anything . . .

As I zoomed away, I checked the rearview once more.

The van was gone.

48: JESSICA

Mom was waiting for me when I walked through the front door. She stood in the kitchen doorway, arms crossed over her chest, her jaw tight. As if I were a teenager and had stayed out long past my curfew.

What is it now? I felt tension coiling like a snake in my stomach.

"Is something on your mind?" I asked.

"You haven't kept your promises to me, Jessie."

I set down my purse and tote bag on a chair. "Mom, I'd love to get a clue of what you're talking about."

"All you care about is your failing little business." She made a broad, sweeping gesture as if to encompass the entire world in her arms. "My kitchen faucet is leaking. My house is still half-painted. It's an embarrassment! You promised to address these things *weeks* ago, and you've done nothing but host a perpetual pity party for yourself."

Talk about walking in front of the firing squad.

"Why're you so upset all of a sudden?" I asked. "And it hasn't been *weeks*, by the way. It's been maybe a week, give or take a day or two."

"I trusted you to keep your word." She wagged her finger at me. "Same ole child of mine. Promising to deliver the moon and the stars. You're so much like your father it's as though he never passed on."

As I stared at her, she turned on her heel and marched into the kitchen. My ears rang from the viciousness of her accusations.

But the events of the past few hours had worn me out. Waiting so long to talk to a detective, high on adrenaline when I finally got my shot with her, getting gut-punched by her refusal to help, and then almost encountering Lance while snooping near his house had left me a bundle of frayed nerves. I wanted nothing more than to open a bottle of wine and relax.

But I couldn't shrug and hope this problem with Mom would go away on its own. Sighing, I shuffled into the kitchen.

Mom had knotted a pink bath towel around the leaking faucet head, some makeshift, lame plumbing fix of hers. The towel looked damp. Meanwhile, she opened the dishwasher, lifted out a dirty plate, and shook at it me.

"These dishes are filthy," she said. "You didn't run the washer last night, did you?"

The task, one of the household duties that I had promised to do as a condition of my living there, had slipped my mind.

"I'll run it now," I said. "Sorry."

"Clearly if I want things attended to properly around here, I have to take care of them myself."

I crossed the kitchen. "I said I'll do it, Mom. Relax."

"Don't bother." She dumped detergent into the washer and slammed the door loudly enough to rattle the floor.

"I'm sorry, but I've had a lot on my mind. I promise to take care of the faucet, the painting, whatever else needs to be done. First thing tomorrow, I'll make some calls."

She let out a harsh, grating laugh, then walked out of the kitchen without acknowledging anything I said. I felt as if we were trapped in a time warp: This felt exactly like unwinnable arguments I used to have with my mother when I was a kid. She would march from one room to the next, forcing me to chase after her, pleading my side of things, while she fired off snarky comments and mocking laughter.

I wasn't going to chase her this time. As I heard her stomp around the house like a petulant child, I approached the leaky faucet, the towel dripping water like blood.

"I'll fix it myself," I announced, to an empty kitchen, but as I looked at the faucet, I knew I couldn't. I had no idea what I was doing, and I was too exhausted to figure it out.

From wherever she was, I thought I heard Mom laughing at me.

49: JESSICA

Growing my business had suddenly become a *lot* harder.
When I moved back in with my mother and got serious about building my freelance marketing consulting firm, things had come easily, at first. People returned my messages and calls, responded enthusiastically to my sales presentations, and eagerly signed contracts.

But ever since I discovered Lance's sabotage, business had taken a turn for the worse—even with new prospects outside of town, companies Lance never would have touched. It was as if the tides of commerce had shifted against me.

That next morning after my visit to the police station, I was scheduled to meet a prospect in Fairburn, a town about half an hour northeast of Newnan. The prospect was a microbrewery seeking to expand brand awareness of its craft beer via a social media campaign.

It was raining again that morning, and I'd skipped my visit to the high school track to use the elliptical in the garage. I got dressed and outside to my car a full hour ahead of my appointment time, knowing how Atlanta-area traffic was always three times worse in the rain.

My car wouldn't start. The BATTERY icon blinked on the electronic dashboard.

Impossible, I thought. I'd bought the car brand new, and it was less than two years old. Didn't batteries last longer than that?

Rain pounded the windshield.

My mind looped back to my secret visit yesterday to Lance's house, me spotting his van in my rearview mirror and peeling away. What if he had known it was me? What if he'd decided to strike back by tampering with my car?

Are you going to blame that man for everything now, Jess? Why not blame him for the rain, too?

I opened the Ring app on my phone. The cameras were offline, again. They had been offline frequently, lately, an issue I meant to look into further, but I just hadn't had the time.

I certainly didn't have time now—I needed to be in Fairburn in fifty-five minutes.

Covering myself with an umbrella, I hurried back inside. Mom was upstairs in her bedroom. She was already dressed and applied makeup in front of her mirror, humming happily to herself.

We'd barely interacted after yesterday's argument, but she seemed to be in a better mood.

"My battery died," I said. "Can I drive your car? Jumping it doesn't make sense because I'll probably have the same issue after I finish my meeting in Fairburn."

"Hmph." She unscrewed the cap on a tube of lip gloss, applied it to her lips, puckered. "You haven't been following the maintenance schedule, have you, Jessie?"

Count on Mom to use this incident to take a dig at me. I tried to hide my irritation.

"My car is only two years old," I said.

"I have an appointment at my primary care doctor this morning. My annual physical exam. I'll need my vehicle. Sorry, dear."

"Uber it is, then." I pulled my phone out of my purse and turned to go.

"Have you made your calls to address our housing issues?" Mom asked. "As you promised to do *first thing this morning*?"

My chest tightened. "I'll take care of that when I get back. I've got a business presentation this morning."

"Of course, *your* business takes precedence." Mom smiled thinly, something hard and unpleasant glimmering in her eyes. "Then you'd better be on your way."

The Uber took fifteen minutes to arrive. Traffic worsened beyond the original drive time estimate due to a wreck on the highway, and despite having GPS, the driver got lost en route.

As it became obvious that I would be late for the appointment, I called my contact person at the brewery, but no one answered. I left a voicemail anyway.

Can this get any worse? I thought.

When the Uber driver dropped me off at last, twenty minutes late for the meeting, the brewery manager informed me that my contact had called out due to a sick child at home.

I'd traveled all that way for nothing.

50: JESSICA

Instead of immediately requesting another Uber and heading back home, I decided to put my time in Fairburn to good use. When life hands you a lemon, make lemonade, right?

The microbrewery was in the town's bustling business district, along a stretch of several blocks populated by local shops and restaurants. Gripping my umbrella to ward off the rain, grateful I had worn comfortable shoes, I trod along the sidewalk and visited one store after another, doing cold pitches at each one.

It was an exercise in self-inflicted torture. I passed out plenty of business cards, but couldn't land any interest in a follow-up meeting. By the time I finished working both sides of the street, my face hurt from smiling and my voice was raspy from delivering my spiel.

For lunch, I had pizza at a pizzeria, after the manager there turned down my sales pitch, but at least he was pleasant about it. A pepperoni pie, and a pint of cold beer. I was supposed to be fasting, but after a brutally disappointing morning, I craved comfort food.

An hour and a half later, an Uber took me home.

As the driver pulled near the house, I saw three vehicles parked in the driveway: mine, my mother's car—and Lance's black cargo van.

He was back.

51: JESSICA

I was still sitting in the back of the Uber, staring through the rain-smeared window at the van parked in the driveway. The vehicle's rear cargo doors faced the house, the same way Lance parked when he was there to work.

"Ma'am?" the driver asked. He twisted in the seat to look at me. He was a young man with a peach fuzz mustache and looked no older than sixteen, but his profile in the app stated he'd been an Uber driver for seven years. "Is this the right address?"

"Do you see a black van parked in front the house?" I asked.

Frowning, he glanced from the driveway back to me. "Uhh, yeah. Is there a problem or something?"

I only wanted someone else to confirm it was real and that I'm not dreaming or completely insane yet.

"There's no problem." I put on a smile I didn't feel at all and reached for the door handle. "Thanks for the ride. Five stars for you, sir."

I got out of the car, a cold rain drizzling from the wounded afternoon sky. The driver hesitated to pull away, as if worried I might do something nuts like set the van on fire.

I waved at him, indicating all was well.

When he was gone, I pivoted to face the house, angling my umbrella over my head. Warm light glowed in the front windows. It was the picture of domestic tranquility, worthy of a postcard.

I adjusted my tote bag strap on my shoulder. Drew a deep breath.

There could be any number of reasons why Lance had returned, but none of them made any sense to me in a rational world. Not after everything I had shared with Mom.

What if he was there against her will? Keeping her hostage in the house?

I almost wanted to believe that was the case, as terrifying as the possibility might be. It was better than the more likely alternative: Mom had reached out to Lance and invited him to come back. Despite everything.

Such a powerful surge of rage welled up in me that I felt dizzy.

She better not have done that. She better not.

Walking those twenty paces from the driveway to the front door felt like the longest walk of my life. I shuffled slowly, carefully, and when I reached the veranda, I lowered the umbrella, collapsed it, gave it a good shake to cast off the water.

As I reached for the smart door lock to type in the access PIN, Lance opened the door.

He wasn't smiling. He wore a grim expression.

"Thank God you're here, Jessica," he said. "It's Mom—she collapsed. I'm calling 911 right now."

52: JESSICA

The brazen absurdity of Lance referring to my mother, yet again, as "Mom" didn't register with me.

All I could think was: *She collapsed* . . .

That couldn't be right. I must have misunderstood.

"She what?" I asked. My tongue felt like a clump of paper in my mouth.

Instead of repeating himself, Lance put his phone to his ear.

"I'm reporting a medical emergency," he said. "A woman very close to me has collapsed and she's still unconscious. Please send help ASAP. Here's the address . . ."

As he spoke to the 911 dispatcher, he turned away from me and strode into the kitchen, his boots thumping across the floor, tool belt jangling.

I couldn't move. My feet felt stapled to the area rug.

My thoughts came sluggishly: *Mom's not in the living room. Is she in the kitchen? Where is Lance going?*

Then: *What did he do to her?*

I rushed into the kitchen.

At first, I saw a bouquet of white roses standing prominently on the island—then I saw ceramic shards scattered on the tile, ringed with a dark pool of spilled tea or coffee.

Then I saw Mom.

She lay on the floor next to the island, on her back. Her eyes were shut. Lance knelt beside her. He tucked a throw pillow from the sofa underneath her head.

"Get away from her!" I shrieked.

In a blink, I was next to her, trying to shove Lance out of the way —it was like pushing against a brick wall. He edged backward with his hands raised in a do-no-harm gesture, or else I might have attacked him.

"What did you do to her?" I screamed. "Why were you here?"

"I stopped by to apologize, brought flowers," he murmured in a soft, reasonable voice. "She didn't want to let me in, but I begged her, and she gave in and asked me to repair the kitchen faucet. She was drinking tea when she collapsed, Jessica. I've called 911 like you've seen, and now you're here, thank the Lord. Paramedics should be here soon."

. . . *asked me to repair the kitchen faucet* . . . The fix I was supposed to take care of, but kept procrastinating to do.

He's lying, about everything. That's what he does.

But this wasn't the time for a debate. Mom was still unconscious, and I searched for a pulse. I discovered a dangerously slow throbbing in her neck. Her chest rose and fell, but barely.

I clasped one of her hands in mine. Her grip was cool and limp as a doll's. I squeezed her fingers gently, pressed my lips against them.

"Hang on, Mama," I whispered. "Please, hang on. You're gonna be fine, Mama. Please, God . . ."

Hot tears blinded me. It seemed to take forever for the ambulance to arrive, but it was actually just a few minutes before I heard the warble of an approaching siren. Lance muttered something about "letting in the paramedics," and I didn't argue with him. I adjusted the pillow underneath my mother's head and held her hand.

"Please, God," I prayed.

She couldn't die like this. Life couldn't be this cruel.

The siren fell silent. I heard multiple sets of footsteps enter the house, men's voices speaking rapidly but calmly. Through the din, I heard Lance say, "I'm a close family friend, guys. She's like a mother to me."

That sonofabitch!

The paramedics filled the kitchen—three men in dark blue uniforms with warm, tired eyes and efficient hands. They moved around Mom with practiced choreography, checking vitals, asking questions in soothing tones. A stretcher materialized. Equipment bags rustled. Lance hovered behind them, hands resting on his tool belt.

And he was smiling that empty smile of his. *Smiling.*

"Get out of our house!" I screamed.

I rocketed to my feet and launched myself at him. One of the paramedics tried to grab me, hold me back, but I moved too fast. I smacked Lance across his handsome face so hard that his head snapped sideways. Spittle flew from his lips and spattered the wall.

"Ma'am, please," one of the medical crew said. "It's going to be okay, please—"

His eyes vacant, Lance turned back to me and smothered me in a bear hug that I was powerless to escape. He was too big, too strong. Keeping my arms pinned against my sides, my face mashed against his chest, he rocked me back and forth gently, as if trying to comfort me. The scent of his cologne filled my head. He lowered his mouth near my ear; I smelled his hot, mint-scented breath wash over me, and felt his cheek press against mine, the sensation disgustingly intimate.

"Get off me!" I screamed, but my voice was muffled by his shirt.

"Shhh . . . it's gonna be all right now, Jessica," he whispered, his lips close to my ear. "I told you . . . I always finish the job."

I screamed and struggled to break free. He suddenly released me and gave me a shove. I lost my balance and tripped over a chair, slamming hard against the floor, the impact sending a spike of agony through my tailbone. I cried out.

"Ma'am, please!" one of the paramedics said. "Stay calm. We're taking your mother to the hospital. She's got very low blood pressure."

"I'll come along," Lance said. "I can ride in the ambulance with you guys."

"Like hell you will." I grabbed the edge of the kitchen table and struggled to stand, pain tearing through me. "I'm her daughter, dammit." I pointed at Lance, my hand shaking. "He's no one to her. He's a snake! He's behind all of this!"

"I need you to stay cool," another paramedic said. "For your mom's sake."

"*I'll* ride in the ambulance," I said.

The paramedic gave a curt nod. They had lifted my mother onto the stretcher. "Let's head out."

I had the presence of mind to grab Mom's purse, which would contain her ID and insurance card.

As we filed toward the front door, Lance's voice followed us: "See you at the hospital, Jessica."

The rain hit my face, cool and clean after the suffocating kitchen. The ambulance sat in our driveway, back doors open, interior lights harsh and clinical. They loaded Mom inside with practiced efficiency. I climbed in after her, my hand finding hers again.

Behind me, Lance stood on the veranda. Watching. Still smiling.

The doors slammed shut between us.

53: JESSICA

Being in the ambulance with my mother unconscious felt surreal, like the worst nightmare I'd ever had come to life. I'd never been in an emergency vehicle, either as a patient or a companion.

While I sat in the back beside Mom, the paramedic on the other side of her, the driver navigated traffic in the driving rain. The wailing siren made my head spin.

But I tried to block out everything and focus solely on Mom, holding her hand, as if I could will her to good health by sheer concentration, and desperate prayers.

The medic skillfully inserted an IV into her hand. Mom resurfaced to consciousness briefly, blinked weakly. My heart lifted.

But within seconds, she passed out again.

Please God, I prayed. *Bring her back.*

The paramedic asked me a question. His badge read DAN. Maybe in his early thirties, he had a beard, a soft voice, and kind eyes.

It was so noisy, I leaned forward and asked him to repeat the question.

"Does your mother take any blood pressure medications?" he asked.

"She has for years," I said. "Lisinopril, I think?"

"What's the dosage? How many milligrams?"

I knew little about Mom's health—she was so defensive, refusing to discuss ailments for fear of being called feeble or senile.

"Sorry, I don't know." I shook my head. "Do you think she took too much and that explains the low blood pressure?"

"Possibly." His brow furrowed.

"She uses a weekly pill organizer. She fills it up every Sunday night. I've seen her use an app on her phone to track whenever she takes her meds—she's very consistent."

I didn't want to tell him my suspicion: That Lance had drugged her. Given her too much of her own medicine, ground it up and slipped it into her tea.

I always finish the job . . .

"What did she do today?" the medic asked. "Any exercise, strenuous activity?"

"She drove herself to the doctor's office this morning. She was fine until I came back."

"Could also be dehydration." He checked her pressure and looked grim. "She's at seventy-two over forty-five."

My heart hammered. Normal range was one hundred twenty over eighty, a benchmark I'd exceeded myself according to my last checkup. She was dangerously out of the healthy range.

"But y'all can help her?" I asked. "She can come back from this?"

"No promises, but she's got a good chance if she's in decent health. The doctors will tell us what's going on."

He wanted her driver's license and insurance card, and I dug them out of her purse and gave them to him. He typed the data into a tablet. It seemed to take forever to arrive at Piedmont Newnan Hospital despite drivers pulling over to allow the ambulance to pass. I fired off several text messages, feeling as if I was operating on autopilot.

Mom hovered on the edge of awareness—I felt her slightly squeeze my hand, once—but she didn't wake up.

When we finally arrived at the hospital's emergency entrance, I tried to get out of the way as they lifted her stretcher out of the vehicle and rolled her inside. I had a million things to do—calls to Mom's primary care doctor and our family, for starters: Junior, my aunt. Mitch—he would want to know. Claire, too.

"I got here as fast as I could," Lance said, suddenly striding behind me as I trailed the medics inside, the men pushing Mom's stretcher. Lance carried a black leather portfolio under his arm.

I whirled. "Get out of here!"

He ignored me, brushed past me. Both of us hurried inside, but with his long strides, he reached the emergency department's front desk before I did. A receptionist rose.

"I'm authorized to make health decisions for Mrs. Marilyn Taylor." Lance zipped open his portfolio, removed a document with an official-looking seal on it, and slid it across the desk to the receptionist. "Here's proof."

"What?" I blinked, stupefied. "*I'm* her daughter!"

"*Estranged* daughter," Lance said smoothly to the young woman. "Jessica here is nothing but trouble. Marilyn specifically asked me to keep her away in case of an incident like this."

"No!" I screamed.

The receptionist studied Lance's document.

"That's a fraud!" I shrieked. "He's a con man! She barely knows him!"

I knew I sounded out of my mind, hysterical, but I couldn't hold back.

"He's just a handyman!" I shouted.

"Typical disrespect for blue-collar workers." Lance shook his head. "You'll see that my health authorization is signed by Marilyn and properly notarized. Everything's in order, ma'am. I've been a close family friend for decades. She's like a mother to me."

"He's lying!"

The receptionist looked sympathetic as she turned to me, but she shook her head.

"You'll have to go to the general waiting area, ma'am."

"No! No! No!"

I lunged at Lance again, and he didn't try to defend himself as I pounded my fists against his broad chest. Two security guards grabbed me and dragged me away to the exit while I shrieked.

"Go home," they warned. "We're ordering you to leave the premises, ma'am. Possibly you can return when you've calmed down."

I stood out in the rain, screaming.

54: JESSICA

Tears streaming down my cheeks, in a state of complete shock, I took an Uber back home from the hospital, clutching Mom's purse on my lap.

A slow, persistent rain continued to blur the afternoon.

I needed to make calls. I needed to do *something*. But too much had happened for me to immediately process. Lance's takeover was so sudden and complete, it had left me feeling powerless.

When the driver dropped me off at the house, I shuffled to the front door. I reached for the smart lock keypad and couldn't remember the stupid PIN. I tried the master code Lance had given us when he first installed it, without success, before I remembered that I had changed it to a new series of digits. I punched in the code and the device flashed green.

I dragged myself inside and collapsed on the sofa, too exhausted to stay on my feet.

The only sound was the rain drumming against the roof. Without my mother present, the house felt abandoned. Was this what it would feel like if she—

Don't you dare think about it, Jess.

I tilted my head back against the cushions and gazed at the ceiling, at that new fan Lance had installed—one of the first tasks he'd completed after he invaded our house. If I'd had the energy, I would have taken a sledgehammer to it. But what difference would it have made?

I stretched out across the sofa. I started crying again. This time, the tears came in a powerful, overwhelming wave, pouring out of me in a hot torrent, dampening the cushions. My entire body shuddered, as if I had a fever. I buried my face against a throw pillow. The fabric smelled faintly of lavender—Mom's beloved fragrance.

I cried myself to sleep.

55: LANCE

I had waited weeks for this opportunity.

To isolate Marilyn and me, alone, in a private patient room in the emergency wing while she fought for her life. The door was shut, blocking the boisterous chaos of the busy hospital— muffled voices from the nurses' station, the squeal of a gurney's wheels on linoleum, someone's television playing a game show.

Inside this cramped room, antiseptic tang hung in the recycled air. Fluorescent panels hummed overhead, casting everything in a sickly pale glow. Machines beeped in steady rhythm—the cardiac monitor tracking Marilyn's struggling heart, the blood pressure cuff inflating and deflating every fifteen minutes with a mechanical hiss. An IV stand stood beside the bed, clear fluid dripping through plastic tubing into the catheter taped to the back of her mottled hand.

Physicians, nurses, and other staff had cycled in and out at various points, in a valiant effort to stabilize the old woman. Someone had examined her bloodwork earlier, frowning at the numbers on his tablet—her blood pressure perilously low at seventy-eight over fifty-two, potassium levels elevated, kidneys not filtering properly. The lisinopril overdose was doing exactly what I'd calculated when I slipped it into her tea. They'd started aggressive IV fluids, pushed medications to support her failing cardiovascular system, and drawn blood to track her body's slow collapse.

Maybe Marilyn would survive this crisis; maybe she would expire like so many of the others before her.

Regardless, the outcome didn't matter to me.

My own pulse remained steady—sixty-four beats per minute, the same calm rhythm I maintained during any job. No trembling fingers. No dry mouth. No cold sweat beading my temples. I cared only about getting her signature. A real one. Not the forged version I'd used to create the fake "health authorization" document I had flashed at the hospital reception desk. The clerk had barely glanced at it before buzzing me through over Jessica. People rarely looked closely at paperwork that appeared official.

But with Marilyn's legitimate signature on a Durable Power of Attorney document, I could execute the rest of my tasks, undeterred, and no one could stop me. The DPOA would grant me full, legal authority to make healthcare decisions on her behalf, to access her financial accounts—to do whatever I wanted with her assets. Everything I needed, wrapped in one legally binding document that would hold up in court, ironclad.

All according to plan.

Jessica had tried her best to derail me, but she was out of her league. Amateur moves, predictable reactions—calling her ex-husband, that clumsy attempt to involve the police. In the end, I always finished the job. Twenty-seven targets over ten years, and not one had escaped the systematic web I'd spun.

I needed only for the old hag to be somewhat conscious. Lucid enough to hold a pen, to scrawl her name across the signature line. Nothing more.

I got my wish after a tech took a blood sample. The young woman—barely twenty-five, SHANICE printed on her employee badge—had moved with practiced efficiency, snapping on purple nitrile gloves, wrapping the tourniquet around Marilyn's skeletal upper arm, tapping at the crook of her elbow to raise a vein. The needle slid in, dark blood flowing into the vacuum tube with a whisper.

Marilyn fluttered awake, scowling vaguely at this physical intrusion. Her eyelids peeled open like old paper separating, revealing cloudy irises that struggled to focus. A weak sound emerged from her throat—not quite a moan, more like air escaping a deflating tire.

"Sorry, ma'am, I'm all done," the tech said. She gathered her supplies and left the room, the door whooshing shut behind her.

Marilyn licked her cracked lips. She was weak, hanging on by a fraying thread, her chest rising and falling in shallow, labored breaths.

I stepped to the bed and touched her arm. The skin felt cool beneath my fingertips, papery and loose over atrophied muscle. She didn't seem to register my presence at first, a vacant look clouding her eyes.

I cleared my throat. "I'm here for you."

The sound penetrated whatever fog swirled through her head. She shifted, the hospital bed's mattress crinkling beneath her, and squinted at me. Her eyes were like weak coffee, watery and unfocused.

"Junior?" she asked. Her voice was raspy, little more than a whisper.

Why bother to correct her? She'd been going senile before any of this happened anyway, her memories already disintegrating—calling me by her dead husband's name multiple times, confusing decades, asking the same questions on repeat. And her confusion would make my task easier. Much easier.

I let my features soften into what I knew looked like concern. "Yeah, I'm here, Mama," I said, pitching my voice lower, gentler. The lie tasted like nothing in my mouth.

"Oh . . ." She blinked, each movement seeming to require enormous effort. "Where's . . . Jessie . . ."

"Jessie stepped out to make some calls." I had already unzipped my leather organizer and grabbed the documents I'd prepared days ago. The DPOA form was pristine, printed on heavy paper, properly formatted with all the legal language intact. I produced a black ball-point pen. "She'll be back soon. Listen, Mom, the hospital needs you to sign some paperwork." I rolled my eyes dramatically, injecting weary exasperation into my tone. "You know how these places are— you could be on your deathbed and they still want to see your ID before they operate."

Marilyn's forehead creased into deep furrows. Confusion flickered through her eyes.

I placed the pen in her trembling hand before she could process what was happening. Her fingers seemed skeletal, knuckles swollen with arthritis, skin mottled with age spots. The pen fell out of her feeble grasp, tumbling onto the white bedsheet.

I picked it up, my movements patient and unhurried. I wrapped her cool fingers around the pen's barrel again, applying gentle pressure to make sure she gripped it properly. Then I positioned the document on her lap, the paper clipped to a standard aluminum clipboard that I'd brought specifically for this purpose.

The visible portion of the authorization showed only a signature line, "Principal's Signature," printed beneath it in Times New Roman font. I had covered up the rest of the document with a blank sheet of paper, obscuring the actual text: *Durable Power of Attorney*. She didn't need to see what she was actually signing.

"Take your time." I placed my thumb on the signature line so she could see exactly where the pen needed to go. "This is important."

She hesitated for a beat, something in her eyes sparking. Awareness? Some primitive survival instinct breaking through the haze of hypotension and medication? Her gaze drifted from the document to my face, searching.

"It's critical for the hospital to have this signed and on file," I said, my voice calm and authoritative—the tone people naturally obeyed. "Or else you might be stuck with a million-dollar hospital bill when this is all over. You don't want that, do you?"

Something that looked like fear surfaced in her gaze, cutting through the confusion. Her breath quickened, shallow puffs through parted lips. Financial ruin—that terror was universal, especially for elderly people on fixed incomes.

She murmured a phrase I didn't quite catch—might have been "no" or "help me" or nothing coherent at all. But she slowly, very carefully, scribbled her signature. Shaky lines. Letters leaning at odd angles. But legible enough. Marilyn Taylor, each letter formed with agonizing concentration, her hand trembling so badly that the pen skittered across the paper.

When she was done, she dropped the pen like it had burned her. It bounced once on the mattress. She collapsed against the pillow, her body going limp, as if the minor act of signing her name had exhausted her. Her eyelids fluttered closed.

I studied the signature against the copy I had on file; the sample from our contractor agreement, when I'd first gained access to the house. Her signature looked good enough. Nice and legible despite the tremor. The letters matched: that distinctive capital M with its exaggerated peaks, the way the T in Taylor curved with a dramatic flourish at the top.

I'd need to get the document properly notarized, but that was a simple task I would take care of that evening. I knew mobile notaries who worked around the clock and didn't ask questions, who'd stamp and sign anything for the right cash payment. Very soon, I'd have complete control over Marilyn's healthcare decisions, her bank accounts, her property. Everything.

I unclipped my phone from my belt holster and sent a quick message to my contact.

Ready for next steps. Meet me at HQ tonight.

Within ten seconds, my contact responded with a thumbs-up emoji.

I felt my chest swell with satisfaction—not triumph, exactly, but the soothing pleasure of a job executed with clocklike precision, the way I liked it.

I glanced at Marilyn. She had already passed out again, her breathing shallow and rapid, the blood pressure cuff inflating with its automated hiss. The machine beeped as it registered her numbers: eighty-one over fifty-five.

Still critically low, but stable enough to keep her alive. For now.

I slipped the signed document back into my leather organizer, zipped it closed, and stood. I'd monitor the situation here for a while longer and then take my leave.

Everything was proceeding exactly as planned.

56: JESSICA

I awoke to someone ringing the doorbell. Disoriented, I sat up and looked around.

I'd fallen asleep on the sofa. How long had I been out? Grayness filtered through the curtains, and shadows filled the living room.

I glanced at my phone. The time read half-past four. In my notifications, I saw several calls and texts from Junior, and Mitch—who I'd recently labeled "Coward" in the Contacts list.

The doorbell rang again, followed by a sharp knock. I hurried to answer.

It was Mitch.

"Dammit, where were you?" he asked. He looked disheveled in a windbreaker, with a Braves ballcap askew on his head. "I've called, texted."

I wiped my grainy eyes. "They kicked me out of the hospital."

"I'm so sorry." His gaze softening, he came inside and hugged me.

I squeezed him hard, grateful for the contact.

"I burned up the highway to get to the hospital as soon as I got your message," he said.

I'd been so out of it that I didn't remember calling or texting anyone, but I must have done that in the ambulance, out of some sort of automatic crisis reflex.

"They wouldn't let me see her," Mitch said, "but when I said I was her son-in-law, a nurse took me aside and told me your mom is stable—for now."

I lowered my head and whispered a thankful prayer.

"That asshole, Lance, is in charge?" Mitch said. "How did *that* happen?"

Shaking my head, I shuffled back to the sofa and dropped onto it. Mitch sat next to me. I picked up my phone and read through messages with only a dim memory of sending them. I'd texted Claire about Mom and she responded: *Oh, God. I'm so sorry! Will get to the hospital as soon as I can, please keep me posted. Praying for your Mom! Love you,* and closed it with several heart emojis. Junior left me a voice message and a text, declaring that he was booking a red-eye flight from Chicago and would arrive in the morning.

There were plenty more calls to make. I could call the hospital and demand updates. But I just didn't have the energy.

I dropped my phone onto the table. It landed like a brick.

"What do you want to do?" Mitch asked.

I ran my fingers through my hair, shrugged. "It's over. He's won."

"You don't believe that, babe." He stared at me.

I didn't bother to correct him referring to me as "babe"—I just didn't have the energy to fight anyone, on anything.

"Seems like he's thought of everything," I said. "I've been fighting for weeks, investigating if you can call it that, making a fool of myself. I'm . . . worn out, Mitch."

His sigh was as loud as mine. Gently, he kneaded my shoulders. It was the sort of impromptu massage he used to give me when we were married, during the good times.

I let myself relax and lean against him.

"We've got to find a way to fight this," Mitch said. "We've gotta challenge this ridiculous health authorization. It's obviously fraudulent. Marilyn never would have consented to this."

"That could take weeks. Meanwhile, he's got total control over Mom's welfare."

"Your brother's coming. He called me. He'll be able to work something."

"Yeah, let Junior save the day. Mom would love that. Lance will probably hustle him, too."

"There's a way to win this, Jess. To get this guy out of the picture and nail him. We'll figure it out."

"Or we can break into his house and steal all the evidence we need to land him in prison."

"Sure." Mitch laughed.

I'd made the remark in jest, out of a sense of total futility. But I didn't join in the laughter.

What if . . .

Mitch stopped massaging my shoulders and leaned back, his eyebrows furrowed as he studied me.

"Jess, you were kidding, yeah?" he asked.

I swallowed. My throat felt parched, probably from so much sobbing. "I know where Lance lives. I drove by there."

"Now, you're not thinking sensibly." Mitch shook his head firmly. "I understand you're upset about this situation, desperate. But there's a right way and a wrong way to handle this."

I pushed off the sofa.

Now that the idea had taken hold, I couldn't let it go. Lance was at the hospital hovering over Mom. While he was there, I could break into his house. Search it top to bottom. Gather all the proof I needed to finally force the police to arrest him.

I paced the carpet, suddenly energized.

"It's irresponsible," Mitch said. "You'll go to jail."

I pivoted to face him. "I want you to go to the hospital. Stay

there. Monitor the situation with Mom as best you can, try to intervene if you need to."

"No." Mitch rose off the couch. "Even if you do this stupid thing
and go to his house, Jess—you *know* this guy has a security system.
The alarm will go off. The cops will come. You'll be arrested for
breaking and entering."

Leaving Mitch to fuss, I ran upstairs to my room and quickly
changed into black jeans, a navy-blue hoodie, and sneakers.

"Jess!" Mitch called. "Talk to me!"

Heading back downstairs, I grabbed a baseball cap out of the
hallway closet and pulled it snug over my head. Mitch stared at me,
fists on his waist.

"I've gotta drive Mom's car." I zipped open Mom's purse, which
I'd left sitting on the coffee table. "I think Lance tampered with the
battery on mine, just to ruin my day."

"Have you listened to a word I've said?" Glowering, Mitch
stormed toward me, but he stopped short of putting his hands on
me. "*Don't* do this. Please."

I rummaged through Mom's purse and located the key fob for
her Toyota.

"If you see Lance leave the hospital, text me," I said. "You're my
early warning signal, babe. I'm trusting you not to let me down."

I stepped toward Mitch and lightly kissed him on the lips. He
continued to glower at me.

"This is a mistake," he said. "You're going to regret it. This won't
improve the situation at all. It's *reckless*."

I opened the front door. Mitch made as if to block me, and then
lowered his arm.

"Dammit, just be careful," he said.

I hurried to Mom's car.

57: JESSICA

The house next door to Lance's was like his: sitting on a large plot of land, surrounded by trees and shrubbery, and accessible only via a long gravel driveway shrouded by elms and pines.

The difference: A weathered FOR SALE sign stood in the front yard, wreathed with kudzu, and the home had a general air of neglect —the real estate market had long forgotten about this place. Knee-high weeds had overrun the lawn, plywood slats covered the front windows, and the gutters sagged underneath a heavy load of fallen leaves.

It looked a lot like my mom's house, actually, if hers had been allowed to deteriorate into ruin. It also was the perfect place for me to hide Mom's car while I broke into Lance's home.

Still, I pulled over to the left to park at the edge of the drive, which I hoped would keep the vehicle mostly out of sight if someone drove past the driveway and looked this way.

I shut off the engine. A slow drizzle plinked against the roof and windshield, and I heard a faraway rumble of thunder.

My heart thudded.

During the drive here, I refused to dwell on the downsides of what I was doing. There were a hundred possible ways this plan could go horribly wrong, but I shut them out.

I couldn't do that anymore. Dire possibilities charged like wild horses through my mind.

You can get busted and go to jail . . .

What if you can't get in, but you're on security camera footage?

What if Lance walks in and kills you?

What if . . .

I picked up my phone. No new messages from anyone.

Would Mitch go to the hospital like I asked and alert me if Lance suddenly left?

How was Mom doing—and how safe was she with Lance in the room with her? Was a nurse nearby?

I started shaking. That was where I really wanted to be—at my mother's bedside, ensuring she had everything she needed. Not out here in the rain getting ready to break into someone's home.

But you're here now, Jess.

I drew in several deep breaths, and my trembling tapered off. But I still felt charged with adrenaline, like I felt right before a sales presentation.

I grabbed my tote bag from the passenger seat and adjusted the leather straps across my chest. If I needed to collect files as evidence, the bag ought to be roomy enough to hold them.

I opened the door—the hinges squeaked like a wounded animal, a sound that seemed abnormally loud in the darkening afternoon. Cold rain sifted inside and peppered my face.

I got out, gravel crunching beneath my sneakers. Quietly, I shut the door.

I put my phone into the back pocket of my jeans, and, just in case, I had clipped a little canister of pepper spray to my waistband. Mitch had bought the spray for me years ago, when news had spread of a rash of vehicle break-ins occurring in the parking garage where I worked, and I'd always kept it in my purse.

But I had never used it, except to test it out once. I hoped I wouldn't need it.

Before I set off, I went to the trunk and used the key fob to open it. The lid squeaked open.

I had never looked inside the trunk of Mom's car, and the volume of random, assorted items reminded me of the condition of the garage. Several pairs of shoes: formal shoes, sneakers, sandals, Crocs. A case of bottled water. A cardboard box that held canned goods, like something she intended to donate to a food bank but had forgotten all about. Another box that held a set of yellowing paperback books. A tangled set of jumper cables. A spare tire.

I found the dusty crowbar underneath the piles of stuff. It wasn't packed in with the wheel replacement kit beneath everything else—probably my mother had thrown it in there at some point, with the vague sense that she might need it someday.

I wrested it out of the trunk—and promptly lost my grip on it.

The tool clanged against the rear bumper and clattered to the ground.

I winced.

Way to be stealthy, Jess. You're a natural at this, aren't you?

I picked up the bar. It was heavier than I expected it to be, but the weight reassured me—it ought to do exactly what I wanted, if necessary.

And what's that? Swing it at someone's head?

I slid the crowbar inside my tote. Carefully, I closed the trunk.

I had everything I needed.

My phone chimed. I slipped it out of my back pocket and discovered a new text from Mitch.

Just got to the hospital. He's still here, I spotted him in vending area. I'm trying to get update on Mom status. Are you okay?

Ready to do what I need, I responded. *I parked next door.*

I switched the phone into Silent mode and set off.

58: JESSICA

Thunder boomed as I crept onto Lance's property. It was almost as loud as my pounding heartbeat.

I'd figured to approach Lance's house from the rear—walking to the front door, in full view of whatever security cameras he probably installed—seemed careless. But a tall, wooden privacy fence surrounded Lance's backyard, the top of it higher than my head.

I tried to open the gate. It was locked, of course.

Sighing, I turned around.

Now what?

At the end of the driveway, a truck grumbled past. I felt dangerously exposed out here, clearly doing something illegal if anyone happened to look this way.

I circled around the perimeter of the fence, to the other side. That gate was locked, too.

But two plastic trash bins were parked against the wall of the house, both of them about four feet tall: one for garbage, one for recycling. My mom had the same setup.

I rolled the first bin against the gate—it was nearly empty. Trash pickup must have been recent.

I laid the second bin, almost empty, on its side, snug against the first one, forming a makeshift stepladder. Climbing on top of it—the surface was a bit slippery—I carefully hoisted myself onto the top of the other bin.

Now the top of the fence was at my knees.

From my new vantage point, I quickly scanned the backyard. There was nothing notable on that side of the yard—only perfectly trimmed grass and a scatter of dead leaves.

I glanced over my shoulder. No one was watching me.

All right. Here goes nothing.

I climbed over the fence and landed on the other side with a jarring thud that reignited a flare of pain in my tailbone from when Lance had shoved me earlier. Wincing, I massaged the aching spot, adjusted the strap of my tote, and turned to the house.

There was a simple concrete patio pad—no handcrafted deck like one might have expected from someone who billed himself as a handyman who could "fix or build anything." No outdoor furniture, plants, or even a basic barbecue grill.

Obviously, Lance didn't entertain or spend any time out here at all.

Keeping close to the wall, I sidled toward the back door. As I got closer to the entrance, I searched for a security camera.

I didn't see one.

Maybe with the tall fence, and the locked gates, he thought it unnecessary.

A set of French doors served as the entrance. The wooden blinds on the doors were drawn shut.

Instead of a keyed lock, he'd installed a smart lock on the door.

That was exactly what I had been counting on. After observing and investigating this guy for weeks, I was getting a handle on how he operated.

He liked to keep things simple. Clean. Consistent.

Mitch had worried about how I'd get inside, without triggering an alarm, and I knew I could use Lance's own methods against him.

The PIN to the smart lock matched the one he'd set up at my mother's house. The tiny indicator light flashed green.

I was in.

But as soon as I opened the door, the security system started beeping.

59: JESSICA

A familiar cadence of beeps echoed through the shadowed house. I recognized it as the same chirping sound of the alarm system he'd installed at Mom's.

I had forty-five seconds to find the control panel and shut it off. If not, the alarm would start wailing, the monitoring company would contact Lance—and from there, the police would be on their way.

Patterns. He does everything the same way, every time.

I had the flashlight app on my phone already on. I swept the light beam around.

He lived like a Spartan. I saw barely any furniture; the few things in there were clean and shiny.

I spotted a basic dinette table in the kitchen, with only two chairs. No dishes or clutter.

No people. No pets—a narcissist like him wouldn't have wasted energy caring for another living creature.

Panning the light ahead of me, I dashed down the main hallway toward the front door, my sneakers squelching across the gleaming hardwood floor.

No photos hung on the walls. No artwork.

Only a simple chair in the living room and a small television on a stand.

The place was as sterile as a lab.

I found the alarm system's control panel on the wall near the front door.

Twenty seconds left, and counting.

I typed in the same PIN he'd set up for the system at Mom's, which was the same PIN on the smart locks.

Incorrect entry, the panel declared.

"*No*," I whispered.

The countdown marched on.

Fifteen seconds . . .

Trembling, I stared at the panel. Should I try a new code—and what would that even be?

Ten seconds . . .

You know him, Jess. Try it again.

Slowly, I entered the same PIN as before, thinking I must have fat-fingered the code in my nervous haste the first time. If it didn't work, I was in serious trouble.

After I pressed the last digit, the chirping stopped.

System unarmed.

I let out a heavy sigh, my shoulders sagging.

That was too close. I had to be more careful.

Thunder rocked the afternoon. The house creaked and sighed.

I checked my phone. I didn't see any new messages from Mitch, which presumably meant that Lance was still at the hospital, and I could take my time searching the place.

But I felt pressed to move quickly. The longer I spent here, the greater the possibility that something I hadn't expected might happen.

The hospital wasn't very far at all from Lance's house—so if Mitch warned me he was coming, I'd need to move fast. I preferred to be done with my search before we reached that point.

It was a ranch house, three bedrooms on one level, with a basement. Somewhere, Lance maintained an office that contained his business records, the mother lode of proof I needed to find.

I started searching.

60: JESSICA

I didn't find anything useful in the bedrooms.

The largest one held a king-size bed with white sheets and pillows so smooth it looked as if no one had ever slept on the mattress. An attached walk-in closet held mostly work clothes and one black suit that looked reserved for funerals.

In one other room I found a weight-lifting bench. A steel barbell loaded with an ungodly number of plates waited in the rack.

The other bedroom was empty.

None of these rooms had photos, artwork, or any personal touches to indicate a human being with an actual soul inhabited this place. I'd seen hotel rooms with more character.

But the house was meticulously clean. Zero clutter, no pieces of useful evidence lying about.

I checked inside the attached three-car garage. It was clean as a showroom, and a shrine to every tool imaginable, glittering on the wall in perfect alignment: hammers, screwdrivers, wrenches, drills, and more.

There were worktables and tool cabinets, too.

There was enough space to park two cars, but no other vehicles were parked in here, curiously. Did Lance only ever drive his work van?

At this point, I was betting on finding evidence in the cellar. If not, this entire adventure would have been for nothing.

I found the cellar door on the other side of the kitchen. Unlocked, it opened noiselessly.

I played the flashlight beam ahead and saw white walls, and a polished wooden staircase descending into darkness.

Quickly, I checked my phone. No new updates from Mitch.

I'd been snooping in the house for about twelve minutes. It felt like twelve hours.

Thunder cracked, making the walls tremble. Leaving the door open behind me, I hurried down the steps and reached a smooth concrete floor.

As I had on the first floor, I kept the lights off. I scanned my phone's flashlight around.

The space smelled of lemony air freshener, and the air was noticeably cooler.

The basement was unfinished, the ceiling a mass of pipes and wooden rafters. I spotted a washer and dryer in one corner, and in another, a set of vented folding doors that I was sure led to a water heater closet.

A full-length mirror hung on the wall in a recessed niche behind the staircase, the brass edges embroidered with an intricate pattern. The shimmering glass reflected my anxious face back at me.

I started to turn away and look around again, worried I had missed something, but I paused.

Other than the mirror above the vanity in the bathrooms, this was the only one in the entire house. And wasn't this a weird spot to hang a mirror?

What purpose did it serve? Lance never did anything out of whimsy or impulse.

I stepped closer to it, playing the flashlight beam around the edges. I ran my fingers along the cool brass frame.

The mirror sat on hinges. Like a door.

I pulled, and it swung to the right, revealing a *real* door behind it. *Clever.*

This door was closed, and it didn't have a smart lock; it had a deadbolt. From this side, I saw only the round steel plate with a keyhole in the middle.

I twisted the doorknob, tried to push the door open, but no luck. The deadbolt lock held firm.

I remembered what I had brought. I dug in my tote bag and withdrew the crowbar I'd taken from the trunk of Mom's car.

If I did this, Lance would know someone had broken into his house, but I hadn't come this far to let a locked door hold me back.

I set my phone on the floor, the light shining upward, filling the area with a yellowish glow. Using both hands, my palms clammy with sweat, I worked the sharp, curved end of the crowbar between the deadbolt hardware and the frame.

Wood crackled, loudly. The noise made me wince.

I had never done anything like this before in my life. Someone experienced at this sort of thing probably could have pried open the door in twenty seconds, but it seemed to take me forever to crack it open.

Come on, Jess. You're wasting time!

By the time I was done, several minutes had passed, sweat dripped down my face, and my arms and hands ached. I let the crowbar clang onto the concrete floor amid a small pile of wood splinters from the damaged frame.

This better have been worth it.

Holding my breath, I pushed the door open.

As it whispered forward, I thought I heard a car engine, drawing very close.

Had I really heard that?

I knelt, picked up my phone off the floor.

And I heard, distinctly, the sound of a garage door clambering open.

61: JESSICA

Mitch hadn't texted me.

That single fact kept circling through my mind as I stood frozen in Lance's basement, on the threshold of the hidden room. Lance had left the hospital. He was parked in his garage right now—the garage directly above my head. My early warning system with Mitch had failed completely.

Why didn't Mitch text? Did Lance spot him? Is Mitch okay?

I could have kicked myself. I had left open the door to the cellar, thinking it would help me leave quickly when I was done. When Lance walked inside, he would see the open door and immediately realize someone had invaded his domain.

Stupid, stupid, stupid!

My hands were shaking so badly I nearly dropped my phone. I pressed my palm flat against my thigh to still the tremor, but it didn't help. Fear had burrowed deep into my muscles like something with teeth.

How much time do I have?

I tried to calculate. Lance would need to climb out of his van, maybe grab his laptop bag from the passenger seat, lock the vehicle.

He might pause to check something on his phone, or fiddle with his keys. Thirty seconds? A minute if I was lucky?

Keep moving. Finish this.

I forced my legs to function, panning my flashlight beam around the room in a wide arc.

It looked exactly like a command center from a spy thriller, the kind of setup you'd see in a movie and think, *That's a bit much, isn't it?* But here it was, as tangible as the sweat on my face.

Six monitors dominated the wall opposite the doorway, each one broadcasting black-and-white security camera footage. I recognized two of the angles immediately—one showed my mother's backyard deck and garden, another displayed our driveway. The other four screens showed places I didn't recognize. Other houses. Other locations. Other targets Lance was watching?

A large oak desk stood adjacent to the wall of monitors, its surface cluttered with electronics. I recognized at least three different router models, a network switch with blinking green lights, external hard drives stacked like cards, a massive laptop—easily seventeen inches—with cables snaking from every port.

Mother lode, I thought, trembling.

I took a quick photo of the setup. But that wasn't going to be enough, not by half. I needed *proof.* Concrete evidence that would hold up in court, that would make Detective Fields believe me, that would finally end this nightmare.

My light landed on a big steel file cabinet standing against the wall to my right, industrial gray with four deep drawers. The metal was cold under my fingertips as I grabbed the handle of the top drawer and eased it open.

Files. Dozens and dozens of manila folders, each one meticulously labeled with typed codes. I recognized the pattern immediately: addresses without street names, just numbers followed by initials.

My God, he's cataloged them. He's cataloged all of us.

My mother's was there: *718MT.*

Seven-eighteen was her house number. MT for Marilyn Taylor.

My fingers fumbled as I grabbed the folder and yanked it free. It was thick, contained maybe fifty pages, but I didn't have time to open it to see what Lance had documented about my mother's life. I shoved it into my tote bag, and my hand was already reaching for the next folder before my brain caught up.

Take them all. Take every single one.

But there were too many. Forty, fifty files in this drawer alone? I started grabbing folders with addresses I recognized from my research, the names of women he'd encountered, charmed, stolen from, killed, and sold off the loot.

One label made my blood freeze: *LH.*

Legacy Holdings. His shell company. The one he'd used to operate in shadows for years.

I snatched that folder and crammed it into my bag.

Somewhere above me—directly above me, maybe twenty feet away—a door opened. The sound was muffled but unmistakable, followed by the solid *thunk* of it swinging shut.

He was in the house now.

My heart kicked into a gallop. *How long had I been down here? Three minutes? Five?* Time had become slippery.

I spun back toward the desk, my phone's flashlight beam swinging. Had I found enough to put him away?

I couldn't be sure. The folders were good, but they were paper trails, documents that a good lawyer might argue away. I needed more. To be sure.

The desk had four drawers, two on each side. I yanked open the top right drawer—office supplies, charging cables, an outdated iPhone. Top left—tax documents, utility bills, a checkbook register.

Bottom right.

My flashlight illuminated two hard drives lying side by side, each one about the size of a deck of cards, matte black with small LED indicators on their faces. They were bound together with a thick rubber band.

Backup hard drives. Maybe holding video footage? Evidence too dangerous for him to get rid of entirely.

I grabbed both drives and shoved them deep into my tote bag, next to the stolen folders. The bag was getting heavy, bulging against my hip. I zipped it shut to keep anything from spilling out.

Footsteps echoed across the floor above me. Not leisurely, not casual. Lance was moving with purpose, his steps quick and deliberate.

He's in the kitchen. He's seen the open basement door.

The stairs were right outside the room—fifteen wooden steps leading up to the kitchen, the only exit from this basement. There was no back door, no window, no way out except via the staircase Lance was about to descend.

You have thirty seconds. Maybe less.

My mind raced through impossible scenarios. Rush the stairs and try to slip past him? Hide behind the file cabinet and hope he didn't come all the way down? Climb up into the exposed ceiling joists and pray he didn't look up?

Every option was terrible. Every option ended with me trapped.

I need to hide.

The words materialized with total clarity, overriding my panic. I couldn't fight him—Lance outweighed me by a ton. I couldn't outrun him if he was blocking the stairs. My only option was to disappear into the shadows and pray he didn't search thoroughly.

My flashlight beam swept the room in frantic arcs, looking for any space large enough to conceal a human body. The dehumidifier? Too small. The gap behind the file cabinet? Maybe six inches of clearance. Under the desk? He'd see me immediately if he turned on the overhead light.

Outside the room, then.

The footsteps overhead grew louder, moving toward the basement door.

He's coming.

62: JESSICA

Just as lights flooded the basement, I hid inside the water heater closet.

Inside the cramped, shadowed space, it was warm and stuffy. The heater hummed behind me, the vibration passing into my bones.

I peered through the door's narrow horizontal slats, my attention fixed on the staircase about fifteen feet away. I tried to stifle the sound of my breathing.

Lance didn't immediately charge down the staircase. As if he was trying to recall whether he had forgotten and left open the basement door on his own, or if he was carefully weighing his options to confront his intruder.

If he found me, he would kill me. There would be no negotiating for him to spare my life—for him, allowing me to live was too risky.

He could claim he killed me in self-defense. I had broken into *his* house, after all. The law would be on his side.

He didn't even need to stage an accident.

Don't let him find you, Jess.

In my fevered thoughts, I played out what I would do. Lance

would come down the stairs, glance around, see the mirror in place but the wood splinters lying on the floor beneath it, and rush into his command center, concerned about what the intruder had done. While he was distracted in the secret room, I would dash to the stairs and flee the house.

He would hear me racing up the steps, but he wouldn't catch me. I was confident I could outrun him—all that time training at the track was about to pay off for me.

Footsteps thumped down the stairs.

I tensed, watching.

My world tilted upside down when I saw the identity of the person entering the basement.

It wasn't Lance.

It was Claire.

63: JESSICA

I gasped when I saw my best friend of over thirty years come down into the basement. If it hadn't been for a clap of thunder at that exact moment, she would have heard me and spotted me instantly.

It couldn't be Claire. The Claire I trusted with . . . everything? What was she doing *here*?

She wore a navy-blue jacket, jeans, and sneakers. A black University of Georgia cap was snug on her head.

She was carrying a weapon; one I recognized from when she'd shown me what she carried in her purse: It was a Taser.

Details arranged themselves in my mind, forming a gut-churning picture: She had parked in the garage, hadn't she? Like someone who had the right to be there, who knew this place intimately.

Claire and Lance together? All along?

I couldn't make sense of it.

She swept her gaze around, eyes narrowed with suspicion. But her attention flicked past the utility closet where I hid.

She pivoted to the big mirror behind the staircase, let out a cry of surprise, and hurried toward it. She pulled away the mirror frame and vanished inside the room beyond.

My phone vibrated in my pocket, and that unexpected notification delayed me for just a heartbeat as I started to open the folding closet doors. I had to check it.

From Mitch: *Lance rushed out of here. Looks like someone called him. Are you still there? Get out!*

Claire had called him, I realized.

The hospital was less than five minutes away.

I stashed my phone and unclipped the can of pepper spray attached to my waist. Finger on the trigger, I opened the utility closet doors.

At that same instant, Claire came out of the hidden room. Our gazes locked.

We had been like sisters for decades, with rarely a moment of silence between us when we were together. But neither of us spoke now.

She aimed the Taser in my direction, and I had the pepper spray pointed at her, too. But we were too far apart for either weapon to do any damage.

The silence stretched on for another second, my entire body tensed.

Then I ran to the staircase.

Claire came after me.

She worked out, too. Harder than I did, and she had done it for far, far longer—outrunning her wouldn't be easy.

I pounded up the steps, two at a time. Breath roaring in my ears, my tote bag swinging from my chest, batting against my legs.

When I reached the top of the staircase, I felt sheer agony plug into my back. I tumbled forward into the kitchen and hit the tile floor on my stomach.

When she entered the house, Claire had switched on the lights in the kitchen. In the harsh glare, I saw the pepper spray clatter out of my fingers and land several inches away, near the refrigerator.

I tried to crawl forward toward it. The effort felt like crawling underwater.

But my thick hoodie had protected me from getting a full blast of voltage from the Taser. If I hadn't been wearing it, I wouldn't have been able to move at all.

"I begged and pleaded for Lance to leave you guys alone," Claire said, coming up the steps behind me. "It's bad business to shit where you eat. But you and him are a lot alike, Jess—pit bulls. Neither of you idiots knows when to let go."

I closed my hand over the canister as her footsteps landed on the kitchen floor.

"I . . . never expected this from you," I said, my voice shaking.

"Did you think he could do it all on his own? He's good, but he's not *that* good, sister."

She kicked me in the hip—hard. I let out a thin cry of pain, tears coming to my eyes.

"Turn over and give me that bag, bitch," she said. "Lance will figure out what to do with you when he gets here."

I didn't move, gathering my strength. "You're gonna let him kill me? After all we've been through?"

"It's only business, Jess. I love you, but I'm not going to prison for anyone. Now, turn over or I'll give you another shot—"

I rolled over and mashed the pepper spray's trigger. The stream of liquid caught Claire full in the face.

She screamed and staggered backward, colliding with the counter.

"You bitch!" She pawed at her eyes.

I struggled to my feet. My hip burned, and the shot I'd taken from the Taser had left me weakened.

Like a drunk, I stumbled to the hallway.

Claire might be down for a few minutes, but what about Lance? I couldn't get trapped in the house with him.

I scrambled to the front door, not the back. In my state, I couldn't scale the fence in the backyard.

I flung open the door.
Ahead, Lance's van veered into the driveway.

64: LANCE

J essica would destroy everything, if I allowed it to happen.

Years of preparation, organization, planning, and execution. A pristine reputation I'd built over decades of valuable service to the community. A fortune I'd amassed from acquiring properties from clients no longer fit to care for them.

I would not allow Jessica the pleasure of ruining me.

I clenched the steering wheel as I turned into my driveway and saw her at the front of *my* house.

Claire had warned me about Jessica from the start. My business partner offered sound advice on the topics for which she was the expert—estate law and the ins and outs of the legal world—but I knew how to handle my clients, especially the challenging ones.

Elimination.

It was always the final step. Closing out the books. Finishing the punch list. It was neater. Cleaner. No one left to mount a challenge, to protest a deed transfer or a sale. To spread negative word of mouth once they had regrets.

Elimination.

Jessica believed she was different. The dutiful daughter, determined to intervene in affairs that didn't concern her. I should have handled her much sooner. That had been my mistake.

It was time to clean up my error.

I hit the accelerator.

65: JESSICA

The van's headlights swept over me as I burst through the front door, the beams catching me like searchlights pinning an escaping prisoner.

I regretted parking Mom's car at the neighboring house, hundreds of yards away. With every movement I felt a hot spike of pain in my hip, agony that radiated down my thigh.

Stupid, stupid, stupid—parking so far away had seemed clever earlier, when stealth mattered. Now it might cost me everything.

But I had no choice but to run for it.

It had grown darker outside as afternoon bled into twilight. Rain pounded the day, and thunder rolled, crashing across the sky like a gigantic bowling ball hitting an epic set of pins.

I launched off the veranda. My shoes hit the wet lawn and immediately slipped—that sickening moment of lost traction. My arms windmilled. The tote bag swung wildly, nearly yanking me sideways. I caught myself inches from eating mud, my heart slamming hard.

Move, move, move!

The bag jostled against my side with every stride, the straps cutting into my shoulder and neck, throwing off my rhythm. But I couldn't drop it. The evidence inside represented everything. Maybe it represented my life itself.

Behind me, gravel crunched and popped. The engine's bellow rose to a shriek.

I risked a glance back.

The van had left the driveway, bouncing across the lawn. Lance hunched forward in the driver's seat, his dark shape visible through the rain-streaked windshield. His posture was eager. Hungry.

He's gonna mow me down like roadkill.

Ten yards left to the tree line. The woods separating Lance's property from the neighbor's stretched ahead—vines, branches, darkness, safety.

My hip shrieked with each stride, but I ignored it, lowering my head, pumping my legs faster. *Faster.*

The van ate up the distance. I felt the engine's heat on my back, felt the disturbed ground shuddering beneath my shoes. The smell of exhaust mixed with wet earth and rain.

I burst into the trees with a cry I didn't remember releasing.

Vines slapped my face. Branches clawed at my arms, their dripping leaves trailing across my neck like cold fingers. I felt delirious with adrenaline and terror and the sheer need to survive.

A glance back: The van skidded to a stop, tires spitting mud, barely avoiding a tree trunk.

Don't slow down. He won't stop.

This was a battle of wills. It had always been a battle of wills—from the moment he'd appeared at our front door to do the first repair. He was as relentless as I was. Neither of us would quit.

Mom's car waited ahead, visible through the thinning trees. If I reached it, if I could just get the engine started and drive away, I'd head straight to the police station and slam the evidence onto the detective's desk. *Now go arrest this guy, dammit!*

I couldn't let Lance stop me. I would not.

The van door squealed open behind me.

I exploded from the trees and sprinted across the weed-tangled lawn. Mom's car stood only a short distance ahead.

Freedom.

You're gonna do it, Jess.

I grabbed the door handle with both hands and glanced behind me.

Something metal hurtled into my face.

The impact detonated behind my eyes, a starburst of white pain. My vision went sparkly, then dim around the edges. The world tilted sideways.

When did I hit the ground? I didn't remember falling, but I was lying on my back next to the car, rain pelting my face, dampness soaking through my hoodie.

Warmth gushed from my nose, hot and coppery-tasting, leaking between my lips. *Not rain. Blood.* My tongue felt thick and swollen. My head seemed to float somewhere above my body, like a balloon tethered by a fragile rope.

At the edge of my vision, a large adjustable wrench lay in the grass, rainwater beading on its metal surface.

He threw it at me.

Footsteps approached, water splashing. Through the gray sheet of rain, Lance materialized. That vacant smile split his face.

I tried to push myself up. Dizziness crashed over me and I collapsed back down, my arms temporarily useless.

Lance seized the front of my hoodie with both hands and hauled me to my feet. My shoes left the ground. For one weightless second, I hung suspended—

—then he slammed me against the car.

The impact knocked the air from my lungs. Pain cascaded across my back. My vision went black at the edges. Consciousness threatened to slip away, and some animal part of my brain screamed, *Don't pass out! If you pass out, you die.*

He towered over me, a monument of muscle and rage. In that moment he seemed mythological. A giant. A demigod. Invincible.

His hand cracked across my face in a backhand strike.

The blow felt like getting swiped by a bear's paw. My head snapped sideways with enough force to rattle my teeth. I felt my tongue loll out—I had no control over it—and tasted fresh blood mixing with the nosebleed already coating my mouth. The coppery flavor made my stomach heave.

Rain streamed down his stubbled cheeks, droplets catching in his eyebrows.

"You've been far too much trouble for me, Jessica." His breath washed over my face—sickeningly sweet breath mints mingling with spiced meat—and my stomach rolled. "It's time to fix things for good."

A Phillips-head screwdriver appeared in his long fingers. He pressed the business end under my chin, just left of my windpipe.

The sharp metal tip bit into my skin. I felt it puncture—a needle-prick sensation that meant it had drawn blood. A whimper escaped me, a sound I'd never heard myself make before.

This is how I die. In the driveway of an abandoned house with my mother's car right behind me and evidence in my bag, and he's going to kill me with a screwdriver like I'm a home improvement project—

"Get off her!" a man shouted from behind us—a voice I never thought I'd be grateful to hear.

Mitch.

Lance dropped me. I sagged against the car, my legs barely holding me up, drugged on pain and shock.

Yelling something wordless and furious, Mitch swung something. A golf club—he kept a set in his car. The wedge-shaped head whistled through rain-thick air and connected with Lance's skull.

The sound—*thunk*—was like a hammer hitting a melon. Solid. Meaty. Final.

Lance staggered sideways, but didn't go down.

How is he still standing?

Just get in the car, Jess. Now.

I groped behind me for the door handle, but I couldn't look away from the fight. Some horrified part of me needed to watch.

Mitch wound up for another swing. Lance roared—an inhuman sound, something between fury and pain—and lunged. Both men crashed into the grass, limbs tangling.

I wrenched open the driver's door, managed to turn halfway—

Lance made a vicious chopping motion. The screwdriver in his hand came down and buried itself in Mitch's chest.

Mitch's howl of agony cut through the rain and thunder. His body curled up, hands scrabbling at the protruding handle.

No.

But I couldn't save him. Not alone. I'd call for help once I escaped—if I could just get the car started—

I dove into the driver's seat and stabbed the START ENGINE button.

Nothing.

No. No, no, no—

I jabbed it again. The dashboard remained dark.

I screamed and slammed my fists against the steering wheel.

Lance climbed to his feet. A hammer materialized in his hand, pulled from that tool belt he wore like a gunslinger's rig. He charged toward the car.

I hit the START button again—*please please please—*

Lance swung the hammer at the driver's-side window in a wide arc.

Glass cracked in a spiderweb pattern, the sound like ice shattering. I screamed. Lance swung again and the car's engine finally hummed to life as the hammer punched through the glass, fragments spraying over me.

He attacked the window a third time, smashing a gaping hole, but lost his grip on the hammer. It tumbled into my lap.

He thrust his arm through the shattered window. His fingers closed around my throat—thick fingers, strong enough to crush my windpipe, cutting off my air. I gagged, twisted away, couldn't break free. His fingernails dug into my skin.

The hammer.

I grabbed it as black spots swarmed my vision. Shifted gears one-handed while his fingers squeezed. My lungs screamed for air.

I smashed the accelerator.

The car rocketed forward. Lance's arm snapped back through the window and the Toyota crashed into an elm tree at the driveway's edge.

The world spun. I flew forward, not restrained by a seat belt. Airbags exploded with a sound like a gunshot, smacking my already-battered face, and a chemical smell filled the car.

Keep moving keep moving—

As the airbag pressed against me, I fumbled for the gearshift.

Lance ripped open the door and dragged me from the car by my hoodie. The fabric twisted around my throat, choking me. I tumbled onto wet grass, but my fingers still clutched the hammer. Some desperate survival instinct had locked my grip around the handle.

He dropped me onto the damp ground. Bent over me. Both of his hands found my throat.

Pressure built in my head as he squeezed. My vision dwindled to a narrow tunnel. His face floated above me, rain dripping from his stubble onto my cheeks like tears.

Swing.

With all my strength, I swung the hammer at his head.

The claw end connected with a sickening thud. The impact vibrated through my arm, all the way to my shoulder. Blood sprayed hot across my face—his blood this time, not mine—speckling my lips.

Lance's mouth opened in a silent cry. His eyes swam with shock, but his hands stayed clamped around my throat.

He's not letting go. He's just gonna kill me.

I swung again. The hammer rose and fell. I swung it again. And again. And again. My arm worked like a piston, machinelike, each blow landing with a wet thud that I felt as much as I heard. Blood flew in hot sprays. His choke hold loosened at last, but I couldn't stop, didn't dare stop, because if I stopped, he'd get back up, he'd always gotten back up—

"He's done, babe."

Mitch's hoarse voice barely penetrated the haze shrouding my mind. I saw him crawling toward me through the rain-soaked grass, blood smearing his lips, one hand pressed to the screwdriver still buried in his chest. His face was haggard, but his gaze was steady.

He glanced at Lance's body lying still beside me in the grass. Blood pooled beneath his head, mixing with rainwater, spreading like a dark river.

"It's over," Mitch said.

My fingers uncurled from the hammer. It hit the grass with a soft, wet sound.

And then I screamed, expelling all my fear, all my pain, all my anger. My scream went on and on, tearing my throat, until the rain swallowed it and I had no voice left at all.

EPILOGUE: SIX MONTHS LATER

The following spring, on a sun-kissed Saturday morning, I moved out of my mother's house.

It was time to get my own apartment. I was forty-four years old now, and I had never lived alone. With no more husband, boyfriend, or roommates, I needed to experience independent living.

Mom helped me pack. Together, we dropped the last cardboard box into the Honda's trunk. I shut the lid.

"I think that's it, Jessie," Mom said. She put her hands on her hips, smiled at me, and turned to look at the house behind us. "It's always so difficult coming back over here, and now, I've no idea if I'll ever return."

Mom had recovered, fully, from her medical crisis. As I'd suspected, an overdose of blood pressure medication had been the culprit. If not for her overall state of good health, she might have passed on.

After I facilitated a final series of essential renovations, Mom moved into a retirement community and put the property up for sale. She freely admitted the place was too much work for her to maintain.

She'd already gotten two offers. The house was a gem and would make the new resident very happy.

"It was a wonderful home for all of us, Mama," I said.

I pulled her into a long, tight hug. Mom and I had been working on our relationship, this time with professional counseling.

Mom stepped out of my arms and wiped a tear away from her eye. I sniffled, too.

My phone vibrated. I slipped it out of my pocket. It was a text message from Mitch; I'd renamed him in the Contacts list to his actual name and stopped using my snarky nicknames for him.

He deserved at least that much after he'd put his life on the line to save mine, sustaining a puncture-wound from Lance's screwdriver that narrowly missed his heart.

I hadn't killed Lance, though in the desperation of the moment, I had certainly tried. He survived that day with serious injuries, but was fit enough to eventually stand trial. After our battle, police got a search warrant for his house and found everything—proof of fraud, surveillance equipment, files on dozens of women. The folders and hard drives I'd taken helped investigators know where to look, but the DA made it clear: The evidence police recovered legally was what would convict him.

My break-in had been investigated—for several tense weeks, I'd wondered if I'd face charges, too. But given the circumstances and the egregious nature of Lance's acts, the authorities let me off the hook.

Lance awaited trial on charges of fraud and attempted murder, and the case against him was airtight. It would be many years before he tasted freedom again, if ever. On that eventful day at the hospital, he'd even manipulated a weakened and confused Mom into signing a power of attorney. If he'd had time to get it notarized, she might have lost everything.

Lance had been too clever and methodical in his work to ever get convicted of homicide. Regardless, his fraud crimes alone would keep him locked up for the rest of his life.

Claire had accepted a plea deal for assault and conspiracy. Turned out she'd been helping Lance for years—identifying targets, advising him on his schemes. She'd lost her law license and faced years of probation. I finally understood how she'd afforded all those renovations, fancy vehicles, and vacations.

Needless to say, we were no longer besties. Sadly, I wondered if we'd ever been friends at all.

How's business? Mitch's message said.

Booming, I wrote back, and it was the truth. I had rediscovered my mojo and had a full roster of clients. *I've started interviews for my first full-time employee.*

That's wonderful. Do you have any dinner plans tonight? Love to meet up if you're free.

I responded: *If Mom can join us, sure. We're hanging out today.*

Bring her along. It would be great to see her.

"Are you up for having dinner tonight with Mitch?" I asked Mom.

Mom had been looking wistfully at the house. "What was that, dear?"

"Dinner tonight, with Mitch. Will you join us?"

Mom smiled, as if we shared some big secret.

"Mitch and I are *not* getting back together," I said. "We're only friends—we learned we're much better that way."

"I didn't say anything." Mom grinned.

"But you were thinking it."

Mom shook her head, but kept smiling. "I'm proud of you, Jessie. That's what I was thinking."

"I don't think I've ever heard you say that before." I felt myself choking up.

"I've told you that before."

"I'd remember if you did. Trust me."

"Well, I should have said it a long time ago. You've always made me proud, baby."

"Thank you for that." I nodded toward the car. "So. Ready to go?"

After we got inside and I started the car, Mom said: "Mitch is such a sweet guy, though. Is there any chance—"

"Hey, why don't we listen to the radio, Mom?"

As I cranked up the radio's volume and drove away from the house, both of us laughed.

HEAR MORE FROM GABRIEL

Did you enjoy this novel? Visit www.gabrielpiercebooks.com now to sign up for Gabriel Pierce's free mailing list. Mailing list members get advance news on the latest releases, the chance to win autographed copies in exclusive contests, and much more. Your email address will never be shared and you can unsubscribe at any time.

ABOUT GABRIEL PIERCE

Gabriel Pierce lives with his family near Atlanta, Georgia, where he is at work on his next novel. Visit his web site at www.gabrielpierce books.com for the latest news on his upcoming books.

www.ingramcontent.com/pod-product-compliance
Lightning Source LLC
Chambersburg PA
CBHW020124120726
47903CB00007B/2100